# SNOW FIGHT

D0368146

# Tales of a Terrarian Warrior, Book Two

SNOW FIGHT

## AN UNOFFICIAL TERRARIAN WARRIOR NOVEL

## WINTER MORGAN

Sky Pony Press
New York

Sky Pony Press books may be purchased in bulk at special discounts for
sales promotion, corporate gifts, fund-raising, or educational purposes.
Special editions can also be created to specifications. For details, contact
the Special Sales Department, Sky Pony Press, 307 West 36th Street, 11th
Floor, New York, NY 10018 or info@skyhorsepublishing.com.

Sky Pony® is a registered trademark of Skyhorse Publishing, Inc.®,
a Delaware corporation.

Visit our website at www.skyponypress.com.

10 9 8 7 6 5 4 3 2 1

Library of Congress Cataloging-in-Publication Data is available on file.

Cover design by Brian Peterson
Cover illustration by Amanda Brack

Print ISBN: 978-1-5107-1683-4
Ebook ISBN: 978-1-5107-1685-8

Printed in Canada

# SNOW FIGHT

# CONTENTS

# Chapter 1
## A NEW ADVENTURE

Miles swung the Pwnhammer in an arc around his head, impressed by the balance and speed with which it completely wiped out a nearby tree. "Oops," Miles mumbled, looking around to make sure no one saw his Noob move. He collected the wood from the tree, pretending that was his purpose all along.

He had already killed zombies, crushed the Eye of Cthulhu, and defeated armies of goblins. Miles had even conquered the Wall of Flesh, earning him this awesome hammer that would lead to his next adventure.

A few days before, Miles had stood alone, staring at an empty field, longing for a friend. And now, that field was a village, one house for each new companion he had earned.

He had chosen his path as a warrior and, Miles admitted to himself, he was an excellent warrior. But

1

he had already lost his guide and knew that more friends would sacrifice things to help him succeed. Miles found himself wondering: was it worth it? He could have stayed a beginner, gaining achievements, battling goblins and collecting coins. He wouldn't be on his way to becoming an expert fighter, but at least life would be easy. Instead, Miles was off to battle his toughest foe yet: the Corruption. The darkness was already starting to spread, and beating the Corruption wouldn't be easy.

Without a guide, Miles knew things would be rough, but he smiled as he looked at his new friends laughing with each other as they worked. Shelly the Mechanic waved, signaling him to come join them.

"Come on, Noob! Stop playing with that hammer and join the fun!" she called out.

Miles placed the Pwnhammer back into his inventory, not wanting to use up its power on defenseless trees, and joined his friends.

Cedric the Wizard approached Miles as he arrived at the village. "Hi John. What can I do for you today?"

"I'm actually Miles, Cedric. But I'm happy to see you're settling into your new home," Miles replied.

Cedric looked around to see if anyone was listening, then whispered to Miles: "Speaking of Miles, don't tell him, but my last place was nicer. This is okay for a Noob house. Fine workmanship."

Miles tried to keep from laughing. Isabella had told him that the old wizard was losing his mind, but his way with magic overpowered his poor conversation skills. "Don't worry, Cedric. I won't say a word."

"About what?" The wizard looked confused.

"Never mind," Miles said, peeking at the wizard's inventory. "I could use a few magical things. I'm off to fight the Corruption."

The wizard's eyes grew wide and his tone grew serious. "The Corruption, you say? A bit over your head, young warrior." He gazed at Miles studying him as if weighing his abilities. "Your power is strong but untamed."

Miles tilted his chin up defiantly. "I know how to fight and, thanks to my training, I know when to ask for help."

The wizard nodded. "Wise words, young Isaac. Heed them well."

*Isaac? Really? Now he's confusing me with a goblin tinkerer!* Miles was polite enough to keep those thoughts to himself.

"Hey Cedric, do you have anything that could help me in my next quest?" Miles asked.

The wizard handed him a rod topped with a glowing flame. "Try this."

Miles aimed the rod at the sky. "What does this button do?" He pressed it. A ball of fire shot out, knocking Miles back. As Miles fell, the rod angled toward the nearby forest. The fire ball followed the direction of the rod, speeding up and slamming into a nearby tree before bursting into flames.

Shelly and Isaac leapt into action and ran toward the tree to battle the fire. "Don't worry! We've got this!" Shelly called.

"Perhaps the Flamelash can wait until you have more experience," the wizard said, pulling out a scepter topped with a crystal. "For fifty gold, I will give you this Ice Rod. Use it to protect you and to provide light."

Miles took the rod more carefully and pointed it at the sky. Nothing happened. "It doesn't work," Miles said.

"You used up your Mana," the wizard replied. "All magic comes at a cost. You gain more Mana when you stand still and listen to the universe."

John the Merchant came up to inspect the rod in Miles's hands. "That an Ice Rod? Nice. It'll get you places. Do good things for you, too. At fifty gold, it's the best magic you can buy."

Miles handed fifty gold to the wizard and shrugged. "I guess that makes me the proud owner of an Ice Rod, whatever that is."

The wizard wandered off.

"Thanks! It was nice doing business with you," Miles called out to him. Cedric disappeared into his house without a word.

"He's an odd one, that wizard, but he knows his magic," John said. "Just like I know my merchandise. Can I check out that Pwnhammer?"

Miles handed it over. "I know I need it to break a demon altar to help me advance, but I don't know *why* ."

"Easy. A demon altar is a crafting station, but *you* won't use it much for crafting. You want it for what you get from it," John explained, handing the Pwnhammer back to Miles. "The first demon altar you break releases cobalt or palladium ore which you can mine. It's intense and awesome for crafting. Things made with palladium can't explode, and things made with cobalt last longer, so either way you win."

"I could've used both of those in the goblin attacks," Miles said. "I need to be prepared for my next battle, which means I'm off to smash a demon altar!" he pronounced. "Who's with me?"

"What are we off to smash?" Jack the Demolitionist asked as he wandered over. "I'm all about that!"

"Miles wants to smash a demon altar for materials, but I was about to suggest we hit the Hallow first," John answered. "It's a good place to . . ."

"Did someone say we are going to the Hallow?" the dryad Isabella chimed in. "Yes, yes! We must go."

"What's the Hallow?" Miles asked innocently.

"It's only the most magical, beautiful, rainbow-covered, unicorn-filled place in existence," Isabella practically bubbled over with happiness. "And wherever the Hallow is, the Corruption and the Crimson are not. You should go, Miles, and see what you are protecting when you work to defeat the spread of the Corruption."

Miles shook his head. "It sounds pretty, but we have to get good building materials. We have to survive out here, and I need the best weapons we can get."

"I side with Isabella," Shelly said as she walked over, brushing the last of the embers from her cloak.

"I side with Shelly," Isaac said, grinning at Shelly. "What were we agreeing to?"

Shelly blushed. "Oh, Isaac. You're so funny."

"Look, it's all in the same direction anyway," John the Merchant reasoned. "We're wasting time standing here. Let's go and figure it out along the way."

They each grabbed a weapon and a few supplies. Miles was disappointed to see he had spent most of his gold on the Ice Rod and had very few coins to spend. Hopefully he wouldn't need to shop for anything expensive before he earned or found more.

As they walked and argued—Miles in favor of the demon altar battle, all the rest in favor of the Hallow—the weather grew hotter and the air became dry.

"Man, I'm thirsty!" Miles said.

"This is the desert," Jack explained.

Just then a shriek pierced the quiet afternoon air. Without thinking, Miles turned and loosed an arrow in the direction of the sound.

"No!" Isabella cried. "Always look first, shoot second. Now you've made him angry."

"Who?" Miles asked. He didn't need to wait for a response. A vulture, hovering above his shoulder, swooped down for an attack.

Isabella raised a leaf barrier, causing the vulture to retreat and attack from another direction. That was all the time Shelly needed to toss her wrench for a direct hit. The vulture fell to the ground. The wrench returned to Shelly's hand. Isabella's leaf barrier withdrew.

"Thanks, you two. I owe you. We can go to the Hallow first," Miles said.

"Friends don't keep score, silly," Isabella said as she hugged him. "But thanks for going to the Hallow. You won't regret it."

"I hope not," Miles replied, sensing that danger wasn't as far off as the dryad hoped.

# Chapter 2
## PIXIES

Miles kept his distance as he walked past the fallen vulture, even though he knew the dead bird couldn't harm him anymore. As the vulture's body flickered and disappeared, he felt his pack get a little heavier. John the Merchant stopped walking and looked carefully at Miles.

"You look like you gained a little weight," he observed. "About sixty copper coins worth, I'd say."

Miles laughed. "That feels about right, but I'm going to hold onto them for now."

John threw his hands up in mock surrender. "Hey, I was making an observation. You know where to find me if you need me."

As Miles and his new friends trudged along, he noticed that Shelly and Isaac were laughing quietly together. He felt good knowing that his presence in Terraria was helping his friends bond, but it also worried him. He had seen the dangers that lurked everywhere he had been in so far. It seemed that getting too attached could distract a good warrior from his—or her—goal of spreading light and defeating enemies.

Suddenly, he heard a happy squeal. He noticed that Isabella had run ahead in her eagerness to get to the Hallow. "It's real! It's here! Come see!"

John and Miles broke into a jog with Shelly and Isaac following close behind. Cedric ambled, in no hurry. Jack the Demolitionist stayed by the wizard's side.

"What is it? Miles panted as he approached.

The dryad was dancing with excitement. "The Hallow! It's more beautiful than I remembered!"

Miles couldn't believe the colorful landscape he saw: blue grass, colorful trees, and the arc of a rainbow above.

"Pretty, isn't it?" Shelly asked.

"It's nice, but it kind of looks like a unicorn threw up," Miles whispered.

Shelly looked alarmed. "Ew, where? Did I step in it?"

Miles laughed. "No, not literally. It's too sweet for my warrior tastes," Miles replied.

Shelly shook her head. "You talk like a Noob." She turned to the goblin tinkerer. "Isaac, you wanna explain this biome to Miles?"

Isaac adjusted his toolbelt. "The Hallow looks harmless, but it's powerful, and the only thing standing between us and the Corruption. Any one of the creatures you'll meet here, night or day, can eat you alive."

Shelly saw Miles's panic and put her hand on Isaac's scaly shoulder. "Okay, tough guy. I didn't mean you should scare the kid." She turned to Miles. "What Isaac means is that the unicorns and pixies here may look innocent, but they're vicious."

Before Miles had a chance to find out more, John walked over. "So, what do you think?"

"About the Hallow?" Miles asked.

"No, about your options. Have you figured out how you're gonna spend the sixty copper sack that's weighing you down?" John replied, a little too eagerly.

"Maybe!" Miles squirmed, stepping back from the merchant. He thought of Shelly and Isaac's warning. "I could use a new weapon, I guess."

John grinned from ear to ear. "*That's* what I'm talking about." He pulled out what looked like a pair of blue discs. "I'll give you this Code 1 for five gold."

Miles turned it over in his hands. "It looks like a . . . but it can't be . . ."

"It's a yo-yo. What'd you think it was?"

Miles tested it in his hands and spun it out. It slashed a nearby tree, then shot back into his hand.

"Whoa," Miles exclaimed in surprise. "That's not any yo-yo I've seen. It's powerful!"

John took it from his hands. "You break it, you buy it." He placed it back in his pack and pulled out a similar one in black. "Try this one. It's even better."

Miles cradled it carefully in his hand. "What's it do?"

"It's just better," John replied quickly. "For you, twenty-five gold."

Shelly took the black yo-yo from Miles and gave it back to John. "Give him the Code 1 and enchant it." She looked back at Miles. "The Code 2 looks cooler, but it costs five times as much and doesn't do much more damage. You need to be a smart shopper."

John shrugged and handed Miles back the Code 1. "I'll throw in the enchanting for free. 'Cause you're a good friend." He raised his eyebrows at Shelly, who nodded back.

Miles handed over five gold coins. "That's all the gold in my pouch. It had better be worth it." Miles walked off with the yo-yo to practice on a nearby tree. He frowned, wondering if John the Merchant was as good a friend as he had thought. On one hand, John was trying to cheat him, but on the other hand, he was just doing his job. Miles thought as he took out a nearby pink tree with the yo-yo.

A few trees away, Isabella let out another happy shriek. She pointed up a nearby tree. "Miles, Miles! Come quick!"

Miles ran over and looked up. It was a series of tree houses connected by colorful vines. "Wow!" Miles replied, impressed. "Who lives there?"

"Me!" Isabella replied. "Help me get in and I'll tell you about it."

Miles created a staircase that wrapped around the trunk of the tree to the first door.

Isabella led the way up the stairs, followed by Miles, John, Shelly, Isaac, and Jack. "Aren't you coming up, Wizard?" Jack asked.

Cedric shook his head. "Too much to do to waste time climbing trees, young Miles."

Jack shook his head and laughed to himself. "Jack. My name is Jack," he said softly.

Isabella walked around the house, touching everything reverently. "I used to live here. It was built by someone I traveled with a long time ago."

Miles wiped dust off of a nearby table. "How long ago was it?"

"Hmm . . . about . . ." She paused as she counted on her fingers, mumbling to herself. "Let's see, three blood moons, then the age of the Corruption which lasted . . . carry the one . . ." Then her eyes lit up. "It's been about a hundred and three years since I was here last." With that, she darted up to the next room, calling back to them, "Come on! Let's see if anything's changed."

Miles turned to John, feeling confused. "Isabella hasn't been here in more than a hundred years? How old is she?"

"She seems young for a dryad, so I'd guess about 400," John replied

Miles was shocked. "400 years is young?"

John shrugged. "The last dryad I worked with was 536. But she kept giving people dandelions. She was a little crazy, but she had great stories to tell. Plus, I made a ton of coin selling all those dandelions she gave me."

John walked over to a pot in the corner of the room. "Hey. Smash this."

Miles eyed him suspiciously. "Why should I destroy something in the dryad's house?"

"It's a breakable pot. That's what it's for."

Miles shrugged and pounded on the pot with his fist. It broke open, releasing a sack of copper coins and a grenade. "Geez, that's a lot of loot."

"Yup. Don't say I never gave you anything." John winked at him.

"Thanks," Miles said shyly, embarrassed that he ever suspected John would cheat him.

Shelly swung into the room on a vine. "Did you guys hear that?"

The two exchanged a confused glance. "Hear what?" Miles was about to say when . . . *zap!* A bolt of lightning sang past Miles's ear.

"Quick, get to the ground!" Shelly darted past them, followed closely, as always, by Isaac. Everyone scrambled down the tree behind them to join the wizard.

When Miles stepped on the blue grass, he was attacked by a small, yellow light. It flitted past his face and struck him with its tiny, sharp wings.

"Squee! Squee!" The light was teasing him, laughing as it danced around his head.

The wings stung his face as he batted it away. "Get it off me!" Miles called, but no one came to his rescue. He flicked the ball of light onto a nearby rock, stunning it. As it wobbled and dove toward him again, he looked around to see that each of his companions was battling two or three at once. Cedric the Wizard was shooting at them with his Flamelash, which explained the bolt that had almost hit him in the treehouse, while Isaac and Shelly were fighting off six at once by swiping at them with swords.

He looked around for John and thought he spied his clothes lying in a heap on the ground. The pile was surrounded by a dozen dancing lights. Why have they taken John's clothes? Miles wondered. Then he saw the mound move, ever so slightly.

"Miles," the bundle whispered in John's voice. "Use the yo-yo."

It wasn't a pile of clothes at all! It was John under attack. Miles shot the yo-yo toward the pile of clothing. With a *crack*, five lights were sent flying before flickering out. He threw the yo-yo again, hitting four more. The remaining three lights stopped attacking John, hovered, then descended on Miles. He fired the yo-yo again, hitting the final lights, which dropped to the ground instantly.

Miles reached out a hand to pull John to his feet. "Thanks, man, I owe you one," John said, rubbing his neck. His face and arms were covered in red spots where he had been hit.

"No problem." Miles grinned. "Glad I bought that enchanted yo-yo from you."

"You're good with that thing," John observed.

The rest of the group walked over. "Is everyone okay?" Miles asked. They nodded. "Good," Miles said. He was starting to enjoy his leadership role. "What were those things?"

"Pixies," Isabella holstered her sword. "I kind of forgot how evil they can be." She bent down to gather a glowing pile of dust. "But they are useful." She handed the dust to Miles. "That's a lot of Pixie Dust. You earned it."

Miles examined the dust. "What can I do with it?"

"The question is, what can't you do with it?" Cedric the Wizard replied. He always seemed to simply appear when magic was being discussed. "But it's not real magic like mine. Want me to pull a gold coin out of your ear?" he asked hopefully.

"No thanks. I'm good," Miles replied. He put the Pixie Dust in his pack. "I'll save this for later. I'll need an anvil to craft anything with it, won't I?"

"Not necessarily," Isabella replied. "You can mix it with hallowed seeds and a bottle of water to make Holy Water."

"What makes it holy?" Miles asked, intrigued by the name.

"When you are fighting the Corruption, it could be your last chance to keep the world pure. One splash of Holy Water could save the world," Isabella replied.

Miles wasn't used to her speaking so seriously. "Do you think I need to make some now?"

"Do you have any seeds?" Isabella asked.

"Hallowed ones?" Miles asked. Isabella nodded. "No. Actually, I don't have regular seeds either."

"Do you have twenty silver coins?" Isabella asked.

"Twenty silver? That's like 2,000 copper! I only have a little more than sixty copper." Miles shook his head. "That could take forever."

Isabella put her arm around Miles. "Don't worry, little buddy. We'll get you more coins." Suddenly, she got a faraway look in her eyes. "Oh," she cried softly.

"What is it, Izzy?" Isaac asked softly.

"We have a lot of work to do," Isabella replied sadly. "With all of the beauty here, I forgot we are not living in a fairy tale." She leaned against the trunk of the tree house.

Isaac sat next to her. "Is it the Corruption?"

Isabella nodded. "It's coming for us."

# Chapter 3
# IN THE HALLOW

As soon as Isabella spoke, the sand at the edge of the Hallow began to darken and the sky turned to fog. Two nearby cacti groaned as they shriveled into nothingness and were replaced by foul-smelling purple ones.

"Ebonsand," Isabella moaned, sinking deeper into the base of the Hallow tree. "The Corruption is taking over."

Miles touched the sand. It had the same texture as regular sand but it *felt* different. He sniffed. The air smelled dark, like mud and the slimy stuff at the bottom of a pond. He walked a few steps and found himself back on spongy Hallow ground. Here it smelled sweet and comforting, like sunshine.

"How is this happening?"

"It is part of the darkness. If you don't stop the Corruption, it will grow and take over everything that is good," Isaac replied.

"What can we do to help?" Miles asked. "Do any of you have ideas?"

"Well, I think we need to defend ourselves. A spell tome, for one," the wizard replied quickly. "A Crystal Storm, I think. That should protect us from hostile mobs."

Jack agreed, taking Cedric's side. "Spells of protection and some good, old fashioned weapons of destruction."

Shelly shook her head. "You're a demolitionist. You *would* say that. We have to stop the spread by creating things that protect the Hallow. That magic water potion the dryad mentioned sounded good."

"Holy Water," Isabella said softly. "That's in case of emergency," she explained. "For now, we could use lots of Purification Powder." The dryad seemed to gain strength as she thought of ways to keep the Corruption away.

The companions seemed divided into two groups: the ones who wanted to arm themselves to fight here and the ones who wanted to go wipe away the Corruption. Miles saw the value in each, but which needed to be handled first? He stopped to think about the Corruption. If he allowed it to it spread a little, he could go find a demon altar and become stronger. Was it wrong to want to sacrifice a little of the Hallow in order to gain more power? *A strong warrior would know what to do*, he thought to himself. *Matthew would know.*

"Matthew wouldn't have been able to advise you with this," a quiet voice from beside him said. He turned to see John by his side. "I figured that's what you'd be thinking because he was your guide." Miles nodded. "But with all his wisdom and experience, Matthew has never faced the Corruption or gone to the Hallow or battled pixies. But you have."

Miles's eyes widened. "So I'm already wiser and more experienced than Matthew?"

John laughed. "Not exactly. I was just saying he wouldn't be much help. You have to weigh your options on your own." John looked out at the landscape that was slowly changing from light to dark even though it was only mid-afternoon. "But I'd recommend you decide quickly."

Miles nodded and addressed the group. "We have two options. Buy Purification Powder to stop the Corruption from spreading. That will leave us defenseless and cost us . . ." He looked to Isabella.

"Seventy-five copper," she replied.

"Or we can buy a spell tome and gather ingredients to craft a Crystal Storm." Miles looked at the wizard. "That's a weapon that shoots off a cloud of missiles?"

Cedric nodded. "More or less. The spell tome costs five copper, plus a Soul of Light for two silver, and a crystal shard for fifteen silver."

"Sixteen, actually," John corrected him.

Miles calculated the amount in copper coins. "We can get protection for 1805 copper and we can heal the world for 75 copper." Everyone nodded. "I don't have that much cash on me for even one of those options."

John spoke up. "I'm confused. You've been crying poor all day, but didn't you just defeat the Wall of Flesh?" Miles nodded. "Then check your pack. That earns you some serious bank."

Miles had forgotten all about the other drops he earned when he fought the Wall of Flesh. He was so focused on losing Lila the Dryad and saying goodbye to Matthew that he forgot about what he had won in battle. After all, part of the reason he was in this warrior business was for the payoff. He ripped open his pack and dug down to the bottom. Nestled in the corner, he felt a tiny coin pouch. With trembling fingers he lifted the pouch.

"Open it!" Shelly called out.

Miles ripped it open and out spilled ten gold coins.

"Now that's something I can work with," John said approvingly.

For the next hour, Miles worked hard. He crafted the Holy Water—for emergencies only—and while he didn't have enough for the Crystal Storm ingredients, he did buy a few throwing knives from Jack and a Dao of Pow from John for extra protection. Then, armed with the Purification Powder, he asked his friends to stand back. "Let's try this stuff out, shall we?"

Miles threw the powder across the scarred ebonsand. Instantly, the cacti turned green and the dark sand lightened.

Isabella closed her eyes and breathed in the warmth of the clear desert air. "It is good. We are getting closer to a balance. For now." She turned to Miles. "Keep up the good work!"

The companions broke into relieved laughter. The sound was interrupted by a low rumbling noise. Everyone stopped and looked around nervously. The rumbling happened again.

"What kind of mob is that?" Isabella asked.

Then another rumble, the loudest one yet, came—from Isaac's stomach.

"It's not a mob," Isaac said. "I'm hungry." The entire group burst out laughing again and even Isaac joined in. "I could use some grub myself," John said.

"I bet we can cobble together enough ingredients to cook something special," Shelly suggested. "Let's head back to the Hallow."

They pulled the food out of their packs and threw it into a pile, collecting enough for a feast.

"Now what?" John asked. "We can't eat it raw."

"I have a kitchen upstairs," Isabella reminded them. "A house in the Hallow is free from the

Corruption. As long as my home is here, I'll always have a safe place to go."

"You dryads are smart," Jack said, clearly annoyed. "But you don't have to brag about it."

Isabella blushed. "I'm not bragging, Jack. I'm offering to share it with you. *All* of you."

Jack smiled and grabbed Isabella in a bear hug, catching her by surprise. "On behalf of everyone, we accept! Now let's make us a feast!"

# Chapter 4
## OLD AND NEW HOMES

As his friends prepared the meal, Miles explored around the tree house. There definitely weren't enough rooms up there for everyone. And, though Miles didn't know what creatures roamed the nights in the Hallow, he figured at least one of them could climb stairs. If they were anything like those nasty pixies . . . he shuddered to think of what other cute-named creatures turned out to be vicious killers.

Miles didn't have long to wonder. He heard the sound of hoof beats, then a grunt and whinny and guessed that something like an angry horse wasn't far away. He drew his sword in time to see a large, white creature charge and leap high over his head. It ran a few more steps, stopped, turned around, and pawed the ground, its ears pinned back, nose pointed straight at Miles.

That's when Miles noticed something strange and unbelievable. The horse had a single silver, twisted horn. It was a . . .

"A unicorn! Miles, look out!" Shelly called, scampering down the stairs. The unicorn snorted, pawed the ground again and charged at Miles. Shelly dove off the bottom stair, knocking Miles to the ground and landing on him protectively as the unicorn galloped over them.

"What the heck?" was all Miles could manage to say.

Shelly threw a shovel to Miles. "Dig a hideout. Deep enough to keep you low. Go!"

Miles did as he was told. He dove into the hole and saw that Shelly had done the same thing. The rest of the companions were watching from the tree house, shouting suggestions.

"Confuse 'em with the Dao of Pow!" John yelled.

Miles pulled out his weapon and held it ready to stun the unicorn. He placed his broadsword nearby so he could finish the job quickly. "Anyone else have advice?" Miles called up to his friends.

"Look out below!" Isaac called, throwing down a spiky ball. It rolled to a stop not far from Shelly's dugout.

"Thanks, Isaac!" Shelly called out.

The unicorn looked recharged and ready to fight. "That first pass was a warning shot," Shelly told Miles. "We'll be fine unless it decides to call its friends."

As if in response, the unicorn reared back and pawed the air. With a loud shriek, the unicorn let out a call that sent Miles cowering into his hiding space. "Are you scared?" Shelly asked.

"Yes," Miles admitted. "But that is a warrior's way of getting ready for battle," Miles said bravely. "My heart is racing, my blood is pumping, and I'm ready for action!"

"Well said, young Miles!" Cedric called down from the tree. Not only was it a compliment, but the wizard even got his name right. Miles beamed proudly, but he didn't have time to reply. Two more unicorns appeared at the top of the hills, one on either side of him. He held his Dao of Pow ready, his finger poised above the button. He had to get the timing right to hit all three as they passed overhead.

They charged forward, two from one side, one from the other. A moment before they passed overhead, Miles pressed the button, deploying the flail.

*Zap!* Three direct hits!

A lone unicorn tried to raise itself up into the air, but with the confused debuff, it reversed down and up. He dropped to the ground and landed on the spiky ball the goblin had dropped.

The battle was going well. Miles and his group had already taken out one enemy and the other two were wandering around confused. Shelly and Miles had their weapons ready. One unicorn wandered past their hiding spots, saw Miles hiding in the hole, and looked ready to attack again. But since it was still dazed, it lifted its head up instead. Miles saw his opening. He swung his broadsword at the unicorn. The beast took damage but was still standing. It shook off the last of the confusion and focused more clearly on Miles. Miles hit twice more, each time causing more damage. The unicorn pawed at Miles with its powerful hooves.

Shelly tossed her wrench, hitting the unicorn from behind. The unicorn whirled to refocus its attack on Shelly. Miles took the opportunity and destroyed the beast. There was no time to celebrate—two new unicorns appeared on the hill. "It's too much!" Shelly called. "You're too inexperienced to take on this many. We'll have to call the others."

Miles shook his head. "I'm the leader. I can do this," he said bravely. "Stay down and I'll take care of them." Miles jumped out of the hiding spot, catching the attention of the three unicorns. "Come get me!" Miles shouted. He used his flail again, stunning them. The three unicorns, dazed by the debuff, collided as they tried to separate. Left was right and right was left for them, but Miles only had a few seconds before the confusion wore off. Broadsword in hand, he plunged his sword toward the nearest unicorn, then slashed at the one next to him. The third, trying to attack, was backing up right toward where Shelly was hiding. "Look out!" Isaac called down.

Shelly threw her wrench, hitting the unicorn on the head and knocking into its horn. Reeling in pain, the beast flailed wildly, knocking Shelly's wrench as it tried to return to her. The wrench clattered to the ground a few feet away from the beast.

"Drat!" Shelly cried out. "That's my best weapon!" She climbed out of the hole and dashed toward her wrench. She was counting on the debuff to keep the unicorn confused.

A few steps away, Miles slashed at the other two unicorns and felled them at almost the same moment. "Oh yeah! Double down!" he called out in triumph.

He looked over to see Shelly had almost reached her wrench. The unicorn shook its head clear of the confusion and focused on the mechanic. "Shelly, look out!" Miles called.

Shelly looked uncertain whether to retreat to her hiding spot or reach forward for her wrench. She lunged toward the weapon. The unicorn leapt toward her. Shelly realized her mistake and raised her arms to her face protectively. "Nooooo!" Isaac called out from above.

The unicorn landed fully on Shelly. Miles surged forward with his sword and slashed at the beast. Miles knew that though he had beaten the unicorn, he was too late to save his friend.

While they crowded around where Shelly and the unicorn had been, John collected the coins, horns and Blessed Apples the unicorns had dropped when they were defeated "Not a bad haul for a quick fight," he observed. "Four Blessed Apples. Impressive."

"Where's your sympathy, Merchant?" Isabella yelled accusingly at John. "We lost our mechanic."

"We lost a friend," Miles corrected her.

Isaac climbed slowly back up to the tree house. "I hope no one minds, but I'd like to be alone."

"She was a good ally," Cedric observed.

"And a good fighter," Jack added.

"I sure will miss her," Miles said sadly. "But we'll think of her fondly in her new land."

"Without a mechanic, we won't be able to set traps. It'll be tough fighting the Corruption without her," Jack said. "You should get to town to meet Shelly's replacement."

"I guess you're right," Miles said. "But I'd like to build a house here first. Isabella was right, it's not totally safe in the Hallow, but we're safer from the Corruption, and there aren't enough rooms up in the tree house for all of us."

Isaac came downstairs. "Might I make a suggestion?" They all nodded. "If we build it right here where Shelly fell, it can be a guard station—a gateway to the tree house."

"Let's do it!" Miles shouted, happy to have an easy resolution. He quickly built two houses at the base of the tree, each with two rooms. "Now we'll have enough space for old friends and new," he announced proudly.

Cedric the Wizard walked around the houses. He seemed to be impressed with Miles's skill. "If it were my house, I'd like it in a different shade. Green, perhaps. But it seems sturdy enough to keep out bad creatures."

"I'll take that as a compliment," Miles told the wizard. He looked up at the sky. He calculated he'd have enough time to get to the village before dark. "I'm off to meet the new mechanic. You all stay here. I'll be back as soon as I can."

They all bid Miles farewell. As Miles walked quickly back through the desert to his village, he felt the weight of the Pwnhammer almost calling to him. There was much work to be done breaking demon altars and stopping the Corruption. He had already wasted too much time in the Hallow. It was a beautiful place, but it still wasn't safe, and it wouldn't be, Miles figured, so he might as well head out to do his job.

It wasn't long before he reached the tiny village and sure enough, a light was burning in Shelly's old house. He knocked, and the door was instantly answered by a mechanic who looked strangely familiar.

"Shelly?" Miles asked with surprise.

"Nah, you got the wrong gal. I'm Autumn." She shook Miles's hand firmly. "Nice digs," she said, looking around. "Love the blinking lights."

"Shelly did that. She used to be the mechanic here," Miles replied. "I'm Miles. It's nice to meet you."

"So, Miles, what's your deal?" Autumn asked.

"My deal?" Miles echoed. "I'm training to be a warrior. Fighting the Corruption, getting rid of hostile mobs, that sort of thing. I'm good at killing unicorns and goblins."

"Good for you," Autumn replied. "I'm good at traps and engines. I bet we'll make a great team."

"We can test that out now if you're up for it. I'm off to seek out a demon altar," Miles offered.

Autumn looked at the darkening sky. "We'd better prepare for night travel, in that case."

"That reminds me, I'm low on supplies. I had been planning on buying some wire and wire cutters from Shelly . . ." Miles trailed off.

"No worries. How much coin do you have?" Autumn answered, pulling out the supplies.

Miles gave her a handful. "This should cover what I need. Plus a wrench." He was quickly getting the hang of trading and liked making deals with his companions.

"Here's a good one. It'll protect you from zombies, but it won't protect you from the Corruption. That's what you have to worry about," Autumn said. "You're going to need some strong stuff to fight that enemy."

Miles pulled out his Purification Powder. "I have this."

"Whoa, you can do some serious damage with that." Autumn said. "We should head out to find us some corrupted land and blast it with this stuff."

"Let's go!" Miles replied, making sure all the doors of the village houses were secured against invaders while they were gone.

# Chapter 5
## DEMON ALTARS

Zombies. Of course there were zombies. But why did there have to be so many on the way back to the Hallow? Miles's sword arm was growing tired from defending himself, and he noticed Autumn's defenses were slowing as well. Miles switched back to the yo-yo and took out the three remaining zombies with one hit.

"Gotcha!" he cried, looking around cautiously to make sure that was the last of them. It was getting so dark, Miles could barely see Autumn standing a few feet away.

"That was some zombie swarm," Autumn said. "You're good with that broadsword and yo-yo."

Clear of the zombies, they entered the forest. Not too far in, the ground and sky turned purple, signaling the Corruption had already spread close to home. Miles was worried that his tiny village was in more danger than ever.

"Do you have any other weapons? Your sword is looking worn."

"I have these throwing knives, your wrench, and of course the Pwnhammer, but I'm running low," Miles replied. He quickly repaired his sword, then raised a zombie arm he had collected from last zombie he took out. "I hear this can be useful."

"Good call. Now to search for a cave. Got a torch?" Autumn asked.

Miles lit a torch and held it up. He instantly regretted it. He was staring straight into the eyes of a gigantic coiled-up snake. "The Eater of Worlds," he said quietly. "This is not good."

"Grenades," Autumn called out. "If you have 'em, use 'em!"

Miles threw a handful at the Eater of Worlds as it rose up and headed straight toward him. He hit the mid-section, which split it into two smaller enemies, continuing on their path. A second grenade split a smaller section, and a third hit the head of one, killing it instantly. He pointed his Ice Rod in the beast's path, built a stairway of ice and climbed to the top. He then pulled out his broadsword, glad he had restored it. He slashed at the segments as they passed, chopping the beast into smaller and smaller pieces until he felt the ice melting beneath him. Miles hopped to the ground before the last block melted, slashing at two more segments as they passed.

Autumn sounded like she was having fun, throwing her wrench at the sections and catching it as it boomeranged back. She popped out some grenades with a 50 percent hit rate and started flinging them. "Yee haw!" she called out. "I love fighting."

Miles had to admit that despite the danger, he was having fun, too. There was one last section left. He flung his yo-yo and took out its head. The Eater of Worlds was defeated, leaving behind a treasure bag for each of them.

Autumn and Miles inspected their treasures.

"Even if fighting wasn't fun, this makes it all worthwhile," Autumn observed.

"This is enough to buy more Purification Powder from Isabella," Miles observed. He looked up and spied a cave entrance a few paces from where they were standing. "Let's check in here," he suggested.

The darkness in the corrupted cave felt a little darker and the air was heavier than usual. "Well, we found the Corruption," Autumn said.

Miles gulped. He hadn't had luck with caves in the past. There were always things hiding in the shadows, waiting to attack. "Are you sure this is the only way to find a demon altar?"

"Afraid so," Autumn replied. "Come on." She led him deeper into the dark cave.

The path split into two: a high road and a low one. Autumn went up and directed Miles to go down. As Miles inched his way down the corridor, he was grateful that nothing jumped out at him.

"You see anything?" Autumn called.

"Nope. Just a bunch of big claws sticking out of the ground." Miles brushed past his fifth one and looked down to see them lined up all the way to a bend in the tunnel.

Autumn ran to him. "You Noob! Those are the demon altars!"

Miles blushed and pulled out an axe, ready to smash it.

"Wait!" Autumn placed a hand on the weapon. "Use the Pwnhammer. That's what it's for."

Miles's face grew even redder. In his embarrassment he had grabbed the wrong weapon. Matthew had warned him that hitting a demon altar with any ordinary weapon would cost him most of his health and do no damage to the altar.

"Thanks," Miles mumbled. Raising the Pwnhammer over his head, he shouted, "Begone evil!" He brought it down with a mighty crash, shattering the altar and releasing a message that scrolled across his vision: "You have released cobalt ore."

"Hey, Autumn, I released cobalt ore!" Miles announced proudly.

"You also released two wraiths!" Autumn replied testily.

Miles turned quickly to see two black ghost-like creatures with glowing red eyes hovering near

Autumn. "Why aren't you moving out of the way?" Miles yelled.

"Slow debuff," she said, struggling to throw her wrench at the closest hovering form.

Miles flicked his Dao of Pow at the wraiths, causing them to flee from Autumn instead of attack. He slashed at them with his blade, instantly despawning them both. "Easy peasy," he bragged.

Autumn shrugged off the debuff and resumed normal speed. She stretched. "I never get used to that feeling," she said. "Ready for the next one?"

Miles readied his hammer above two altars, one stacked on top of the other, but then he paused. "Will wraiths come out every time I take out an altar?" Autumn nodded. "More altars at once means more wraiths, right?" She nodded again. Miles weighed his odds. He took out two with one swipe when he hadn't even been prepared, so two sets of two wouldn't be that challenging. He brought his Pwnhammer down, then quickly switched to his throwing knives. He whipped around and pegged each wraith, then turned to Autumn, grinning.

She clapped her hands in appreciation. "You are one solid warrior."

"Thanks," Miles said. "I do think it's my calling." He scooped up the coins the wraiths had dropped as another message scrolled by: "You have released mythril ore. You have released titanium ore."

"This is fun. I'm starting to get the hang of this," Miles said happily, readying his Pwnhammer for the next altar. "I bet I can take out three at once with no problem at all."

"I bet you could, Miles, but remember why we're here," Autumn reminded him gently. "The Corruption is spreading. We won't know how fast until we get back to your dryad, but I do know it is already close to your house."

Miles raised the Pwnhammer again and brought it down on another altar. "I hate this Corruption! I hate fighting an enemy with no face. I kill zombies and goblins and unicorns and creepy floating eyeballs," Miles continued as he slashed another two wraiths and pocketed the coins. He ignored the next message announcing his new cache of palladium ore. "Darkness is just . . . darkness. It's no fun to fight."

Autumn put her hand on his shoulder. "I totally get it, but you've gotten the most you'll get out of these altars for now. With each one you hit, you release less ore than the time before. Our time will be better spent spreading the powder and pushing back the Corruption."

Miles reluctantly put the Pwnhammer away, noticing a map he hadn't seen before. "What's this?"

Autumn looked over his shoulders. "That map shows the entire world. The purple is where Corruption has already spread. The pink is the Hallow." She traced her finger along the line from where they were standing to the beginning of the Corruption. "Oh," she gasped in surprise.

"What?" Miles asked anxiously.

"Isn't that where your house and village should be?" Autumn pointed to a purple spot on the map.

Miles looked at the trail from their position in the cave through the Corruption-filled forest to the valley where his home once stood. "Oh," he echoed. "It's gone."

Without warning, Miles lifted his Pwnhammer and brought it down on altar after altar, yelling out his frustration. "It's not fair!" Smash. "I worked hard!" Smash. "I can't do this anymore!" Smash.

Wraiths flew out at him from all sides and he switched quickly from weapon to weapon, first unleashing his yoyo, next his throwing knives, and finally slashing with his broadsword. Miles saw Autumn's wrench fly past him and take out a wraith sneaking up behind him. He was glad she was sticking by him, despite his outburst of bad temper.

"One left," Miles finally called out and slashed the final wraith as his drop of coins clinked to the ground. "We did it!" Miles announced happily. He expected a cheer from Autumn, or even a reprimand for acting irresponsibly, but there was no response at all. Miles looked around, panicked. "Autumn?" he called quietly. Still nothing. *"Autumn!"* he shouted. There was still no reply. "No." He shook his head in disbelief. "Not Autumn, too."

# Chapter 6
## POWDER IN THE WIND

W hat's all the yelling about?" Autumn said, wiping her hands as she came into view.

Miles jumped up and surprised the mechanic by wrapping his arms around her in a giant hug. "You're okay!"

"Yeah I'm okay," she said, peeling Miles off of her. "A few floating ghosts aren't gonna take me down. I figured you had them, so I took off to get my wrench back. Stupid thing didn't boomerang."

"Well, I'm glad. And you were right, we released enough ore to build as many weapons as we need. It's time to spread that powder. Where do we start?"

"It's easiest to find the edge and beat it back, then dig a trench to contain it," Autumn advised. "Let's see that map."

Miles handed over the map. "Your old village is a goner for now, I'm sorry to say, but if we hit the edge of the forest here," she said, pointing to a spot where purple met green, "and went to the Hallow for more Purification Powder, we'll be in good shape."

Miles and Autumn walked out of the cave. The sun was already rising on a new day. "We were down there longer than I thought," Miles said. He checked the map and pointed to his left. "It's this way, right?"

Autumn turned the map upside down. "No, Miles, this way is right."

"I know that way is to my right, but is it the *right* way? Or is left right?" Miles turned the map upside down then right side up again, clearly confused.

"You're better at weapons than directions, kid." Autumn patted him on the head. "Let me hold the map."

Miles handed it to Autumn and followed her across the dreary, corrupted landscape. "I'm beginning to hate the color purple," Miles complained. "This place stinks like something's rotten."

Halfway through the forest, the trees formed a line, purple on one side, green on the other, as if they were choosing sides in a game. "This is it. The line where the Corruption ends. For now," Autumn announced.

"So this is where we place the powder?" Miles asked.

"Yep," Autumn nodded. "Spread it out, starting at this green tree line, and don't skip a spot."

The powder didn't cover as much ground as Miles had hoped, but already the forest looked brighter and greener than before. "I think we bought ourselves some time," Miles said proudly.

"Your work isn't over yet. Now you dig a big wide trench," Autumn answered. "Dig deep, all along the border between the Corruption and the healthy forest to stop it from spreading."

Miles took out his pickaxe and eyed it sadly. "It's not much of a digging tool. You don't happen to have a drill, do you?" Autumn shook her head no. Miles took a deep breath and started digging.

The sun was high in the sky when Miles finished digging the trench. Autumn eyed it with satisfaction. She checked her map and saw that they had gained some ground over the Corruption. "Nice job," she said. "Now let's head to the Hallow."

"One second," Miles said. "I must have dropped my weapons when I was digging earlier. We have to head back down underground."

Miles spied his weapons near the cave entrance. "Let me grab them and we can head out." Miles had placed his hand on his Dao of Pow, when he heard a sound. He turned to see a giant bug spawn from the edge of a block. He recognized it right away. "That's a clinger." Miles lifted his shield as the bug fired a cursed flame. His shield provided knockback resistance, momentarily stunning the creature and allowing Miles to approach and slice it with his sword. "Hah! Take that!" Miles laughed as he collected the drop of four cursed flames and silver coins.

As he was about to leave, he noticed a wrapped gift that hadn't been there before. He was about to open it when Autumn called him away. "Come on, let's go!" Miles placed the gift in his inventory and went back up above ground.

"How are we gonna cross this gap?" Autumn asked.

"Easy," Miles replied, taking out his Ice Rod and building an ice bridge. "Remind me to thank the wizard when we see him. This is a great tool." Miles and Autumn crossed back into the healthy green forest before it melted. They made their way through the desert and back to the Hallow, passing a few harmless scorpions and picking off a dozen sand slimes along the way.

"This looks like a good place to mine," Autumn suggested. "You need to grab some of the mythril, palladium and titanium ore we released."

Miles didn't have to dig far to grab a hefty cache of ore. "I think this should do it," Miles said, counting his stacks of ore. "We can make a whole arsenal of weapons now."

When Miles saw the rainbow sky and blue grass in the near distance, he broke into a run. "Hey everyone! I'm back!" The group came rushing down the tree house steps to greet Miles and meet the new mechanic. "This is Autumn, our new mechanic," he panted, out of breath from sprinting.

After the introductions, Isabella took Miles aside and whispered to him. "You are making progress, but the Corruption is spreading faster than you are repairing it."

"I was afraid of that," Miles said. "Autumn showed me how to dig a trench around the Corruption to contain it, but not before we lost our village."

Isabella was not surprised. "I know. Our new mechanic is good. Perhaps better than our old one."

Miles felt badly admitting it, but he knew she was right. Shelly was a great mechanic, but Autumn knew about so much more than machines and fighting. She was a great advisor.

As Miles rejoined the rest of the group, someone walked down the tree house stairs and stood, waiting for an introduction. "Oh, Miles, we have a new friend," Jack announced. "This is Asher. He's an adventurer, like you."

"Hey! How's it going?" Asher shook Miles's hand. "It's nice to finally meet you. I've heard so much about you."

"I wish I could say the same about you," Miles muttered under his breath. "I mean, yeah, it's nice to meet you, too."

"I wandered over here after a battle with the Wall of Flesh. I was badly hurt," Asher explained. "Your kind friends took me in and helped me heal.

We traded for lovely items, like Greater Mana Potion and a Crystal Ball."

Miles looked longingly at the items. If he didn't have to spend all his hard-won coins on Purification Powder, he could buy magical items from the wizard, too. For the first time, Miles was regretting his decision to become a warrior.

"Looks cool," Miles admitted grudgingly. "I got cool stuff, too," he announced. He wasn't sure why, but Asher brought out his competitive side. Miles showed off the coins, cursed flames, and other drops he had picked up.

Isaac was most impressed by the zombie arm. "Got any more?"

"Sure, I have three," Miles said proudly. "I can sell one to you."

"Done!" Isaac shouted, dropping four silver coins into Miles's outstretched hand. "Oh, I do love playing with new ways to destroy things!"

"I'm glad to see Isaac is feeling better," Miles whispered to Isabella.

"He was sad about Shelly, but then he got excited to meet the new mechanic," she replied.

"Speaking of new ways to destroy things, anyone want to help me craft new weapons?" Miles asked, knowing he'd catch his friends' attention.

Jack was the first to reply. "You have to make a Mythril Repeater."

"No way," John chimed in. "Save your mythril for armor. A Palladium Repeater deals more damage."

Jack shook his head. "You don't know what you're talking about, Merchant."

"Don't fight." Miles separated them. "I think Mythril Armor is the way to go."

"Good choice, Miles." Asher appeared by his side and peered at Miles's stacks of ore. "That is a lot of rare ore."

Miles positioned himself protectively between Asher and his stash. "I worked hard to get it. You should head out there and see what you can mine for yourself."

Asher shrugged. "I may. Once I've rested." He rubbed his arm dramatically. "I'm still recovering." Asher turned and searched his inventory, pulling out a stack of meteorite bars. "Do you think you could use this?"

Jack pushed Miles out of the way. "Is that meteorite? From a Shadow Chest?"

"Um . . ." Asher stammered, avoiding looking at Jack. "Yeah, I guess." He turned back to Miles. "Since you have a Mythril Anvil and a Soul of Light and Pixie Dust already, you can make a Meteor Staff . . ."

Miles looked sideways at Asher. "How'd you know I had all that?"

Asher shrugged. "Your friends were telling me about all you've been through. I guessed . . ."

"Well, whatever. That sounds cool, but everything around here comes at a price. What would you want for it?" Miles asked.

"I've been staying in your house, eating your food, and enjoying your hospitality without asking," Asher said. "Consider it payback."

"In that case, thanks a lot," Miles replied. He felt bad about suspecting the guy. Asher seemed grateful, but there was something about him Miles didn't trust.

Miles combined the bars with the other ingredients to craft a staff. He weighed it in his hands. "I don't suppose we can try it out . . ."

Isabella stopped him. "Please don't. I'd hate to ruin all these trees with a meteor shower. Besides, you should save up your Mana for when you need it."

"I guess it can wait." Miles shrugged, then turned to crafting a stack of weapons and armor. When he was done, he held up the stockpile for his friends to inspect.

"Not a bad job, young . . . what was your name again?" the wizard asked. "I have trouble with names sometimes. You're the nice adventurer who built me that lovely house."

"Miles," he replied, trying to be patient.

"No, you must have me mistaken for someone else. I'm not Miles. I'm Cedric. I'm a wizard," Cedric answered and walked away.

Miles put away his weapons and sifted through the items he had brought home. He held up one cursed flame. "Anyone know how to use this?"

"You can craft powerful weapons with it," Asher said, ticking the many uses off on his fingers. "Cursed dart, cursed arrow, cursed bullet, cursed torch . . . you can also use it to make a living fire block if you have a Crystal Ball, which I happen to have."

"Isn't that just a piece of furniture?" Miles asked.

"Well, yes. But the other things are great weapons," Asher admitted.

Miles picked up the present he had found back in the cave. It was wrapped, but it looked like it could hold a Crystal Ball. *That would show Asher if I got a Crystal Ball as a gift for being a great warrior and didn't even have to trade for it.*

Miles tore the wrapping to reveal a snow globe. He shook it, but nothing happened. "Isn't this supposed to make snow fly?" *What a rip off,* Miles thought. Not only was it a silly snow globe, but it didn't even do anything. As he held it up to the light, he noticed a smudge on the surface. As he wiped it off, a message appeared: "The Frost Legion is approaching from the east."

All at once, everyone turned to look at Miles. "What did you do?" Jack demanded.

"N-n-nothing," Miles stammered. "I touched this . . ."

"Snow globe!" Cedric shouted. "Quick, nobody panic!"

"What's happening?" Miles asked, confused by all the excitement. "What's the Frost Legion?"

"Let me ask you a very important question, John. Do you want to slay a snowman?" Cedric asked.

"*My name is not John, you crazy wizard.* What are you talking about?" Miles shouted.

Another message appeared: "The Frost Legion has arrived."

"I changed my mind," Cedric shouted. "Everybody panic!"

Miles turned to see a legion of about eighty snowmen marching toward them. "Uh-oh." He called out, "Get ready everyone!"

# Chapter 7
## THE FROST LEGION

The snowmen hopped across the blue grass, jumping and dancing playfully toward them. The only thing was, this idea of play didn't look like it would be fun for Miles and his companions. The snowmen were waving swords, pointing guns, and hurling snowballs with evil grins plastered across their faces.

Miles hit the first few, taking them out with his Ice Rod before his Mana ran out. Isaac, in true goblin form, rushed head-first into the crowd of snowmen, hurling spiky balls and slashing his sword while calling out a battle cry. Isabella quickly threw up a leafy wall of protection while Autumn stood atop a low garden wall, throwing her wrench at the approaching mobs.

Miles switched to his sword and fought alongside Isaac for a few moments, but when Cedric let out a piercing shriek, he left the goblin to check on the wizard. Miles ran toward the source of the wizard's cry, where he found Cedric running around in circles, the back of his cape on fire.

"Nasty fireballs," Cedric exclaimed. "I was hurling them and the snowmen ricocheted my fireball back toward me. "You don't play fair!" He shook his fist as Miles put out the fire. The snowman fired a round of snowballs at them in response.

Miles grabbed Cedric and sat him behind a thick, yellow tree. "Stay here," Miles cautioned the wizard. "Use your fireballs only in case of emergency and only if they don't have shields up, okay?"

The wizard nodded absently as he checked the singed edges of his cape. "Ruined," he moaned dramatically. "It was my favorite."

John backed up into Miles and Cedric as he took out a handful of snowmen with as many knives. "I'll hang out here with the wizard if you want to head back into the action," John offered, holding out a stack of knives. "I can hold them off with these."

"Thanks!" Miles got back in time to see Jack hurling grenades at the oncoming rush of snowmen.

"Take that!" the demolitionist called out.

Miles came alongside Jack and started throwing his yo-yo as the snowmen came closer. "This is harder than fighting goblins," he panted.

"Yup," Jack agreed. "Speaking of goblins, I got this if you wanna help Isaac. His sword is no match for these guys."

Miles patted Jack's shoulder and set off to where he last left Isaac struggling to fight off a wave of enemies. He looked down and saw that Asher was running to his rescue, waving a flail. Miles called out to them: "You guys okay?"

Asher and Isaac both replied with a thumbs-up gesture, so Miles left to check on Isabella and Autumn. The dryad's leafy wall of protection was beginning to waver, and Autumn's wrench was looking worn.

"Help us, Miles!" Autumn called out. "We weren't ready for this attack."

"I'm here to help!" Miles stood in front of the protective wall, took out his sword and swiped at the last few snowmen. The enemies fell. Isabella let her defenses drop and collapsed in a grateful heap. "Thanks!"

All was quiet. Miles looked around and saw that, despite low health, the companions he saw were mostly unharmed. Cedric went up to the tree house to change his cape, while Autumn followed behind to repair her wrench. The dryad went to lie down and Jack came up alongside Miles after tucking away his last few grenades for later.

"How'd the goblin tinkerer do?" he asked. "That guy was crazy, rushing in to slay fifty snowmen on his own. I like that guy!"

"Yeah, he's crazy alright. I'm glad Asher helped out," Miles admitted. "I guess that proves he's a good guy."

"You doubted it?" Jack asked, surprised.

Miles nodded, embarrassed. He looked around to where he had last seen Isaac and Asher. He didn't see Asher anywhere, and finally spied the goblin under a huge pile of snowballs. He didn't seem to be moving. Miles approached slowly, fearing the worst but hoping for the best.

"Isaac?" he asked cautiously. There was no response. "You okay?"

Isaac's form shimmered for a moment, and then he was gone. Miles closed his eyes, trying to hold back the tears of frustration and sadness at losing another friend in battle.

Jack came over and shook his head sadly. "He was one crazy goblin."

Isabella came over. She took one look at the demolitionist and Miles and she knew. "Maybe he's with Shelly again," Isabella offered, hopefully.

"Where's Asher?" Miles asked, looking around.

"I hope he's okay," Isabella said softly. "He ran right into the attack behind Isaac. I hope he didn't . . ."

Jack put his arm around her. "I'm sure he's okay. I mean, I hope he is."

Miles suddenly straightened up, determination in his eyes. "This attack is costing us too much. We are running out of time to fight the Corruption, and now we've lost another member of our team. Maybe two." He turned to Isabella. "Do you have any more Purification Powder?"

Isabella looked up in surprise. It was clear she was still mourning the tinkerer's departure. "Yes, of course. Why?"

"I'm going back out there. I need to build another trench and dig deeper," Miles announced. "With my new, stronger tools and my armor, I can cover more ground." He pulled out a sack of gold coins. "How much powder will this buy?"

Isabella took the coins and handed him several large stacks of powder. "It will buy enough," she said, looking at Miles admiringly. "You are a great warrior, but you also have a good heart. You know the right thing to do."

Miles blushed and bent down to fix his armor, avoiding everyone's eyes. "Yeah, well . . . anyway, I'll be back soon."

Cedric and John approached the group. "Where are you going?"

"Isaac is gone. I'm off to fight the Corruption," Miles announced, glad to have an important job to take his mind off the recent battle.

"You can't leave," the wizard replied, clearly afraid. "If you go, who will save us from the snowmen? They have guns and knives and projectiles. When you get back, we'll be gone just like that goblin tinkerer."

John patted his shoulder. "Don't worry, old wizard. We'll protect you until he gets back."

Miles had an idea. "You can all come with me," he suggested. "This way, if the snowmen come back, we can face them together."

Isabella looked around. "What about Asher? He may still be okay."

Miles took a deep breath and thought for a moment. "If he was taken out, he'll respawn just like Isaac and Shelly. Maybe he'll find us again. If Asher is just hurt, we'll be back soon to help him." He looked at the group to see their reaction. Autumn gave a nod of approval that only he could see. The rest of the group murmured their agreement.

"Well, I guess we all agree," Autumn said. They all went off to grab their weapons and supplies for their next journey.

One by one the group gathered back at the base of the tree house. Miles checked his inventory, making sure he had his trusty weapons that had served him so well, along with the Mythril Armor that had protected him during the goblin attack. Chain mail armor was surprisingly comfortable, and he tried slashing his broadsword a couple of times to test out his flexibility inside the hard metal shell. *Not bad*, he thought. *I'll be ready the next time a wave of snowmen attack us.*

No sooner had the thought run through Miles's head when Isabella called from the top of the tree house, "Look out! The next wave is coming!"

"More snowmen!" Cedric shouted and scampered up the tree to the highest room. "I'll do what I can from up here," he shouted nervously.

Miles readied his broadsword, took a deep breath, and sped off in the direction of the Frost Legion.

# Chapter 8

## THE SECOND WAVE

M iles activated his Dao of Pow, confusing the snowmen that began to surround him and his friends. As the snowmen milled around, accidentally shooting and stabbing each other from the debuff, Miles conferred with Jack the Demolitionist.

"Can you think of any way we can get rid of these guys quickly and efficiently without any more casualties?" he asked.

"I'm glad you asked!" Jack replied. "You'll dig a trench on either side of where we're standing, let the snowmen wander in, then blast them with TNT."

"Won't that destroy the area around us?" Isabella asked, showing concerned for the land.

"It will," John admitted. "But it will save our ammunition and our strength so we can live to fight the Corruption together."

"The demolitionist is right," Autumn reassured the dryad. "It's a good plan."

Miles exchanged most of his shrinking supply of coins for two stacks of TNT, then set about digging a trench to the east and west of his companions. "This should hold them off," he said, wiping the sweat from his brow. "We'll need to fire at them. Keep your ranged weapons ready. They can still shoot at us before they fall into the trap."

Isabella put up her protective wall of vines as Autumn held up her wrench, Jack and John held up their weapons, and Cedric held up his Flamelash from his perch in the tree house.

"Everybody ready?" Miles called out as the snowmen bounced closer.

"Yes!" they all shouted, shouldering their weapons. Miles held the TNT ready as he watched the snowmen approach. The snowmen began to fall, one by one, into the pits he had dug. He peered into the west trench, careful to avoid the bullets and snowballs that were coming from the trapped yet persistent enemies.

"Is it time yet?" he asked. Jack nodded and motioned for everyone to plug their ears. Miles dropped half of the TNT into the west trench, diving away from the explosion toward the other trench where he dropped the rest of it.

It was practically raining snowballs as the army blew apart, defeated. Miles looked around at his stunned companions, who hadn't even needed to fire a shot.

"That. Was. Fabulous!" Isabella said, clearly amazed at the attack. "It was fast, efficient, and brilliant!" She looked down at the fiery holes where the snowmen had been. "Hey Miles, would you mind filling in the holes before we go off exploring again?"

"No problem," Miles told the dryad as he tossed dirt blocks into the pits. He stopped halfway through refilling the east trench. A side wall had opened to reveal a large cave. "Anyone mind if I pop in to take a look around before we go?"

Isabella checked her map. "The Corruption is spreading slowly now. It can wait if you are quick about your business."

"Excellent," Miles said, hopping down into the pit and heading toward the cave. "I'll only be a few moments. I need some coin and these snowmen aren't good for any drops aside from snowballs."

Miles made his way into the tunnel. As he wandered through the silent cave, he was alone with his thoughts and he didn't like what he was thinking. *This is all my fault. If I hadn't rubbed the snow globe, we wouldn't have had to fight the Frost Legion—twice—and used precious resources. And we wouldn't have lost Isaac.* He tripped through a cobweb and stumbled ahead, realizing how dark it had grown. Miles lit a torch and continued deeper into the tunnel. There was no sign of Corruption, so that was good.

Lost in his thoughts, Miles almost tripped over a spider web and instead, fell straight into a web-covered chest. His slime torch dropped to the dusty chest and sputtered out. As Miles lit a new one, he saw a cute little pink-haired girl trying to free herself. "Ew, my hair, there's spider web all over it!"

Miles quickly cut through the webs and helped her out. She brushed herself off and said with disgust, "Don't go exploring with scissors, they said. You won't get trapped in a spider's web, they said!"

"Um, well, you're okay now," Miles stammered. "I'm Miles, by the way. I'm an adventurer."

The girl looked him up and down. "It's a good thing you found me. You are in serious need of a stylist." She reached out and brushed the cobwebs out of Miles's hair. "Did you even try to brush your hair today?"

Miles blushed. "Well, I've been busy. You see, we've been up against these gangster snowmen, and we're fighting back the Corruption, and . . ."

The girl looked behind him. "Who's we? Your imaginary friends?"

Miles was about to get defensive, then stopped himself. "You know, you haven't introduced yourself yet. You haven't given me the courtesy of telling me who is insulting me."

Now it was the pink-haired girl's turn to blush. "I'm sorry. I'd like to say I'm not usually this rude, but that would be a lie." She stuck her hand out toward Miles. "Fresh start. Hi, I'm Sarah. I'm a stylist."

Miles went to shake her hand, but she pulled hers away at the last second. "Ew, I'm not touching those dirty hands. Where have you been?"

"I told you. We were fighting the . . . oh, never mind," Miles said, turning to the chest. "I came here for the treasure, and I've found it. And now you're free from the web so you can go." Miles opened the chest and cursed lightly under his breath. "Oh drat."

"What's up?" Sarah said, peering over his shoulder.

"No coins," Miles said, but he pulled out a Web Slinger and placed it into his inventory. "A worthless trip."

"Hey!" Sarah said, clearly insulted. "Not totally worthless—you met me!"

Miles shot her an annoyed glance. "Yeah? And what can you do aside from insult people?"

"I can . . . I can give you a shave and a haircut! And change your look for battle." She pulled out a bottle of brown dye. "Dye your hair?" she asked hopefully.

"My hair is already that color," Miles pointed out, walking away. "Thanks anyway."

"Wait!" the stylist called after him. "If you're looking for coins, take these cobwebs."

"What would I want cobwebs for?" Mile asked, trying not to sound too interested.

"You can turn them into silk and trade for *mucho* coins." Sarah hopped in front of him. "I don't have my scissors, but I can help you collect them if you want."

"What's in it for you?" Miles asked.

"Do you have a spare room? It's not that I'm lonely, it's just that you could use a stylist to keep your look . . . fresh." She wrinkled her nose with disapproval at his clothes and hair.

"Fine!" Miles said. "We have a spare room at the tree house, but you'll need to help out."

The stylist bounced around the cave, grabbing cobwebs as quickly as she could. "You won't regret it, I promise!"

"I already do," Miles muttered as he placed the rest of the cobwebs into his inventory.

As they were about to leave, something black and squeaky brushed past his hair. Miles shuddered. "What was that?"

"That was a giant bat," Sarah said quietly. "Whatever you do, don't let it hit you."

"Why not?" Miles asked, ducking as the bat swooped back overhead. He tried to wave it away with his slime torch but discovered that was not going to keep this bat away.

"Giant bats give a nasty debuff. You'll get confused and knock yourself out trying to get away while it eats your brains." Sarah reached into her inventory and pulled out a pair of very stylish scissors. "Will you look at that? I had my scissors with me the whole time!" She began hacking at the air near the bat.

Miles placed his torch on the wall, reached into his inventory for his sword and instead pulled out a zombie arm. "Not quite a broadsword, but it'll do the trick," Miles said as he waved the arm at the bat swooping overhead.

"Like, *ew*!" Sarah squealed at the sight of Miles waving around a dead zombie arm. "Put that thing away!"

Miles ignored her and hacked at the bat, knocking it toward the cave wall. Sarah raised her stylish scissors and hacked at the bat's wing.

"Nice job with those things," Miles called out, impressed. He finished the bat off by clubbing it with the zombie arm. It dropped to the ground, leaving behind a handful of silver coins.

"We're a good team, right?" Sarah asked hopefully.

"Yeah," Miles admitted. "You're actually good in a fight."

"Actually? That's not a compliment. That means you didn't expect me to be good," Sarah sulked. "But you're right. I probably come across as all bark, no bite."

"Don't worry about it," Miles reassured her. He was growing to like this fiery stylist. She was funny, even if she didn't mean to be. "Let's head up and I can introduce you to my other friends."

"Other friends?" Sarah said hopefully.

"Oh, come on," Miles said playfully. "Stop fishing for compliments and let's go."

# Chapter 9
## MINING

M iles led the way through the winding cave and took a left turn, straight into a dead end. "Not very good with directions, are you?" Sarah asked.

"I'm so glad you noticed, Sarah," Miles said sarcastically. "Any idea how we can get out?"

"Why do you want to leave now? You came here for coins, so let's find some chests in this dirty old cave." Sarah led the way down a corridor Miles hadn't noticed before. It felt like it led further into the cave, which could help his search for the Corruption.

"What do you want coins for, anyway?" Sarah's voice echoed as she walked into a large, high-ceilinged chamber.

"Purification Powder," Miles replied, lighting another torch. He held it up to the walls to make sure there were no more giant bats lurking in dark corners. "The Corruption is spreading quickly, and it's my job to stop it."

"I thought your job was to be a warrior," Sarah said.

Miles shrugged. "That's how it started. It was my dream when I arrived here. But the more I see of the world, the more I realize that the Corruption must be stopped and I'm the best guy for the job."

"You're a big braggart, you know that?" Sarah observed. "But don't get all offended. I like that about you. You know what you're good at, and you aren't afraid to admit you're horrible with directions." She smiled at him.

"Well, you did catch me in a weak moment. Standing in a dead end and all." Miles held up his torch, lighting up a small alcove in the room. "Hey, I think I found a chest!"

"Lemme see!" Sarah grabbed the torch and looked up close to it. "Yup. That's a chest alright!"

Miles reached out his hand to open it, but the chest had opened itself revealing a set of pointed teeth and a tongue. "Look out! It's a mimic!" Sarah called. Miles jumped back but it was too late. It lurched forward with a chomp. Sarah and Miles backed up into the large underground room, then turned and ran away from it.

"Let's split up," Sarah suggested. "We'll confuse him."

"No way," Miles responded. "I'm not leaving you defenseless."

Hearing that, Sarah whipped out her scissors and slashed at the mimic, slicing off a piece of its outstretched tongue. "I wouldn't say I'm defense-less, Noob."

"Nice," Miles muttered, truly impressed. "In that case, I'll go this way, you go that way." Miles ran off in the opposite direction and the mimic followed behind him. He could see Sarah trying to sneak up on the mimic, and she was about to succeed when he saw something move behind the stylist. "Sarah, look out! Behind you!"

Two armored skeletons had spawned out of nowhere and were moving toward Sarah. She wheeled around and slashed, damaging both of them with one blow. They reeled back, stunned for the moment, but Miles could tell they wouldn't be stopped for long. He fired his Ice Rod, hitting one skeleton right in the chestplate, damaging its armor. Then he fired an ice block straight into the open mouth of the mimic. It closed its mouth and shuddered, clearly surprised.

"Hey look, it has brain freeze!" Miles called to the stylist.

"How can you be funny when we're under attack?" Sarah called out, trading hits with one of the skeletons. "It's all I can do . . . ugh . . . to fight these . . . urgh . . . hostile skellies."

"It's a weird talent I have," Miles said, taking a large leap and landing on top of the mimic chest with a loud bang. Its tongue was hanging out of its mouth as its teeth came chomping down, chopping off another piece of it.

"Way to go!" Sarah called out, stabbing each of the skeletons in turn, first the one on her right, then the one on her left. "If you're done playing with your little monster, can you give me a little help here? It's two against one."

Matt brought his sword down on the chest, slicing it in two for a final defeat. He leapt over the mimic and somersaulted toward Sarah and the skeletons.

"Heads up!" Miles called as he rolled like a cannonball. Sarah dove out of the way as the skeletons looked up in surprise. Miles bowled into them both, sending skeleton bones flying in all directions. He stood up dizzily as the cave spun into view. "Did we get 'em?" he asked.

"Yes!" Sarah replied, jumping up and grabbing Miles in a big hug. "We did it!"

Miles blushed uncomfortably as Sarah backed up. "Sorry, I'm a hugger. You'll learn that about me. Well, I guess you already did." She bent down to pick up what looked like an ordinary sword dropped by the skeleton. "What's this?" She swished the sword in the air and unleashed a beam that crashed into the cave wall.

"Beam sword! Best drop ever!" Miles said, taking it from her. "It's a sword, it's a flashlight, it's a fiery projectile launcher . . . it's three weapons in one!"

Sarah rolled her eyes. "You are weird about your weapons. What else did you get?"

Miles picked up two pouches of silver coins from the skelly twins and a pouch of gold from the mimic, along with a Titan Glove. "Nice! Now I have to get a slap hand, and my knockback will be unstoppable!" He weighed the coins in his hand. "This wasn't what I expected when I came down here, but overall it was a successful detour."

"Is that because of the drops or because you met me?" Sarah flipped her ponytail and laughed.

Miles found his face reddening again. It had been doing that a lot since he entered the cave and he was willing to bet it didn't have anything to do with the cave. "Both, I guess," he replied. "If you can get us out of here, that is."

"No worries at all." The stylist looked left, right, up and down, stuck up her finger to test the wind and sniffed the air, then walked west. "This way."

"You could tell which way to go from doing all those things?" Miles asked, impressed by her tracking skills.

"Nah, I was going that way anyway." Sarah hopped down the corridor, her ponytail bouncing behind her. All Miles could do was follow.

They hadn't traveled far before they turned a corner and were almost blinded by the bright sunlight that greeted them. Before he could check the time, a message appeared: "The Frost Legion is approaching from the East."

"Oh no," Miles groaned. "Not again."

# Chapter 10
## SNOWBALL FIGHT

Sarah looked excited. "I've never met the Frost Legion before. I hear some of them drop cute hats."

Miles laughed. "You would think of fashion at a time like this. Unfortunately, you have to defeat them first." He looked at her scissors. "Do you have any ranged weapons?" Sarah shook her head sadly. Miles handed her a wrench from his inventory. "Just aim and throw, then hold your hand up. It'll come back to you if you do it right."

"I think I can handle that," Sarah said. The two broke into a jog and caught up with the rest of Miles's companions running toward them.

"We heard the Frost Legion is on its way again," Isabella said. "We figured you'd need help."

"You guys are the best!" Miles said. "Thank you for coming. Let's get to that ravine so we can get an advantage over them."

John caught up to Miles and whispered, "Where'd you pick up the stylist?"

"Cobwebs Cave. Watch out for her, she's sassy." Miles grinned.

"I'm only sassy because I care," Sarah said defensively, running up to join them. "And because once all this is over, I'm so giving you a makeover." She turned to look John over from head to toe. "Either you have style, or you get styled. For you, I'd recommend something . . . low maintenance."

John smirked. "Thanks, I think. I'm John. I'm a merchant."

"Nice to meet you. Don't try to sell me anything. I'm not buying." Sarah said.

"Suit yourself. I'm here if you need me." John shrugged and headed toward the hill.

They had rounded the hill to find the snowmen were coming straight at them.

"I hate to bring up Asher, but has there been any sign of him?" Miles asked John. "I thought about it and realized he couldn't have been defeated alongside the Goblin Tinkerer, because there was no headstone or drops where he disappeared."

"I hate to say it, but do you think he ditched Isaac and took off?" John's voice trailed off.

Just then Asher appeared from behind a tree. "You think I did what?" he asked casually. "I heard the snowmen were back so I came to see if I could help this time."

He sounded sincere, Miles noticed. "That would be nice, Asher. Thanks," Miles said, embarrassed for suspecting him of taking off. "Let's get to our battle stati—" *Whap!* Miles's sentence was cut short by a blow to the head with a giant snowball.

Asher was first to spring into action, scooping up the snowballs landing around them and then whipping out a snowball cannon to shoot them back at the intruders. "I'm fighting fire with fire! Or snowballs with snowballs, anyway!" He seemed to enjoy himself, calling out "Yeehaw!" or "Whoopiedoo!" every time he made a direct hit.

Sarah fought alongside these new companions, throwing and catching the wrench with the same skill she applied to her stylish scissors, while the Magician gleefully shot fireballs into the oncoming crowd of snowman with his Flamelash.

Miles took out the snowmen who had gotten through the distant defenses using his yo-yo, but as its power began to fade, he switched to his broadsword, slashing at their round white bodies. Miles reached into his inventory to unleash a heavenly shower of rocks onto the snowmen with his Meteor Staff and realized he hadn't brought any of his new weapons.

As his sword gave out, Asher tossed him a musket. "This should get the last of them," he shouted.

"Thanks!" Miles shouted back, firing the gun into the crowd of evil snowmen. Back-to-back,

Miles and Asher fought off the invaders, high-fiving each other as the last snowman fell.

"I'm glad Asher stuck around for the fight this time," Autumn observed quietly to Miles. "I was beginning to question his loyalty."

Miles didn't want to admit that he was thinking the same thing. "He did a good job. We couldn't have defeated them as easily without him," Miles said simply. He was being honest without openly agreeing with her. "I'm going to go thank him and return his weapon." Miles excused himself as the rest of the team started picking up the snowmen's drops. He noticed Sarah filling her inventory with snowman gangsta hats.

"Hey Asher." Miles approached him as he was picking up the last of the snowballs. "Great job." He held out the musket. "Thanks for the loan. I can't believe I left my new weapons back at home."

"No worries, friend," Asher replied cheerfully.

"It was helpful in the fight. And you were great, too. I was glad to have you fighting by our side. We lost track of you somewhere in the middle of that first wave," Miles said.

"Yeah," Asher replied. "I ran off to get more ammo, and when I got back, you all were gone. Was the tinkerer able to hold 'em off when I left? Where is he, anyway?" Asher looked around, suddenly realizing that Isaac wasn't there. "Did he get hurt?"

Miles shook his head. "Unfortunately, we lost him in the battle. The snowmen overpowered him when you left."

Asher closed his eyes and looked genuinely stricken. "Oh! It's my fault he's gone. I'm sorry." He looked at Miles, searching his face for an emotion. "You must hate me. You must blame me. Do you?"

Miles was uncertain how to respond. "He was one crazy warrior—rushing head first into that battle. I don't think there was much we could do." Miles admitted, realizing for the first time that was the truth. "I don't blame you." He stuck out his hand and Asher shook it gratefully.

"I'm so glad. And I'm sorry I ever caused you to doubt me." Asher seemed relieved. "To make it up to you, I'd like to help you stop the Corruption," Asher continued. "I know you have Purification Powder. I can spread the powder and do whatever it takes."

"We're happy to have you on the team." Miles felt relieved as soon as he said it. He was glad to have the uncertainty out of the way. He hoped he had made the right decision.

# Chapter 11
## WORMS

Miles stood at the top of the hill, looking over the piles of snow where the Frost Legion had fallen. He was proud of everyone. They had fought well and finished off the legion in an easy battle.

"Thank you all for your help," Miles called to his companions. "We have defeated the snowmen—again—but now, we have the Corruption to fight. With Asher by my side, we will work twice as quickly."

"Yay, Asher!" Isabella shouted.

"Let's meet back at the tree house," Miles announced. "When the Corruption is gone, we can enjoy a well-deserved rest."

They applauded. Autumn gave him a thumbs-up of support. Then he and Asher prepared to hit the road.

As they were ready to leave, Isabella came over with the map, showing the spread of the

Corruption. "You'll have to dig deep. Remember, use the Purification Powder from the edges toward the center first, then dig a wide trench, deeper than you think you'll need. The underground Corruption spreads as quickly and in another direction—down."

"Got it, boss," Miles said.

"There's one teensy problem," Sarah said as she walked over. "Mr. Rough-around-the-Edges here has a *terrible* sense of direction. He can't even find his way out of a cave!" Miles winced as she laughed. "It's funny because it's true," she added.

Miles joined her laughter. "I can't argue with the stylist, actually. Fearsome warrior. Good leader. Not great with maps." He shrugged.

Asher reassured them. "Where Miles falls short, I can fill in the blanks. I not only have an excellent sense of direction, I can memorize anything."

"I hope that's true, Asher, because I'm counting on you to get us there and back safely," Miles said cautiously.

"I've got this," Asher said confidently. "And now, we must bid you farewell!" he said with a wave and a bow. "Until we meet in the Hallow!"

The two set off to find the edge of the Corruption. The two walked for a while in uncomfortable silence. They didn't know each other well, and despite all Asher was doing to help, Miles still didn't really trust him.

Asher finally broke the silence. "I really appreciate you accepting me into your group," he began. Miles was certain he was about to ask a big favor. "You have such an amazing group of friends. I wish I could . . ." He trailed off. He looked so sad and lonely.

Miles felt bad for him, and he felt guilty about mistrusting him. "You can stay with us for a bit, if you want," Miles offered.

Asher's face instantly lit up. "Do you really mean it? You're a great guy, Miles. Is there room for me in that great big tree house?"

"I'm sure we can find a place for you," Miles offered.

"That would be amazing. A home is such an important thing to have," Asher said. "You don't realize what it's worth until you leave yours behind."

Miles raised his eyebrows in surprise. Was Asher about to reveal something about his past? "Is that what happened to you?" he asked.

"Kind of." Asher grew silent.

It was clear he didn't want to talk about his past, but Miles pressed him for more details. "Where are you from?"

Asher waved his hand vaguely in no particular direction. "I come from another world, far from here. Like you, I built houses and friends moved in. We traded and fought mobs. They taught me things about magic and the ways of the world. Same as you."

"What made you leave?" Miles asked, genuinely curious. He couldn't imagine wanting to leave his friends and go off completely alone.

Asher walked over to a nearby tree and picked at the rough bark. Miles felt like he was hiding something. "I'm an adventurer like you're a warrior. I have to explore . . ."

"Don't you miss your friends?" Miles asked.

"Sure I do," he said almost too quickly. "Why wouldn't I?" He tossed the piece of bark on the ground, his mood changing suddenly. "Hey, I've never been in this part of the forest before!"

Miles heard a rustling sound and instinctively flattened himself to the ground. "Quick, get down!" he called to Asher.

Asher obeyed, lying face down on the ground next to Miles. "What is it? More snowmen?"

"Not this time," Miles said, looking up. A large, one-eyed bug was circling at a distance. "It's the Eater of Souls."

"That doesn't sound good. What is it and how do we fight it?" Asher asked.

"It's like a giant jumping bug. I haven't fought one yet, but I hear they can hurt you badly," Miles cautioned him.

Asher whipped his enchanted boomerang at the mob, killing it instantly. "Well, that wasn't so bad, was it?" he said smugly.

As if in response, a dozen more bugs appeared overhead and began circling the duo. "Keep that boomerang out," Miles advised. "Ranged weapons will keep them away." Miles grabbed his yo-yo and with one swift stroke zipped it out to slice up the nearest enemy.

"Nice," Asher said. "You definitely are cut out for this!" He tossed out his boomerang and missed, but the weapon came back to his hand for another chance.

Miles repeated the yo-yo trick a few more times until the weapon was spent, then zapped a couple with his Ice Rod. "I shouldn't use up the Mana for these dirty bugs," Miles realized. He switched to the throwing knives and took out the last few enemies. They made sure that was the end of the swarm, then went over to pick up the coins the enemy had dropped. "That's a hefty pile of coins, should we split it fifty-fifty?" Miles asked.

"No way, I only took out three. You got all the rest," Asher protested. Miles waved away his protests and handed him half the coins anyway. "Thanks, man. Now I owe you again!"

Miles looked around, noticing the air and ground had changed without them realizing. "The Eater of Souls only spawns in the Corruption," he recalled. "Somehow we walked right into it without realizing it."

"Maybe it spread as we were standing here," Asher guessed. "Does that mean it's time for Purification Powder?"

"Yes, I guess so," Miles replied, taking out the powder and giving some of it to Asher. "Remember what Isabella said. Start at the edges and go toward the center. Then we start digging."

Asher watched Miles dust the ground. The purple grass instantly turned lush and green. Asher held up a palmful of powder and blew it outward across the purple grass. The powder traveled farther and faster.

"That's neat!" Miles copied Asher's movements, and within minutes they had turned the whole surrounding area green. "Where'd you learn a trick like that?"

Asher shrugged. "I figured it was worth a try." Something in the way he said it made Miles think that wasn't the whole truth, but he let it go. They had a long way to go before their mission was complete.

"Ready to start digging?" Miles asked.

"I'm ready when you are!" Asher replied, taking out a weird tool that Miles had never seen before.

"What is that?"

"Oh this? It's a Laser Drill. Neat, huh? It's the best digging tool around. We can get through the Corruption in no time with this." Asher fired up the drill and it instantly cut through ten layers of corrupted dirt.

"Wowee!" Miles whistled with admiration. "I'd like to get my hands on one of those!"

"You'll have to find a Martian saucer first." Asher said casually.

"You've seen one?" Miles asked.

"No, not me," Asher said modestly. "I had a traveling companion once, like you. She gave it to me. As a gift."

Miles couldn't believe someone would give away a tool that valuable. He put aside his curiosity, though, because he saw there was much work to be done. Miles began hacking the dirt with his pickaxe. It had once been his favorite mining tool but next to the drill, it felt like he was using a wood slab.

They were far down and still hadn't dug out the last of the underground Corruption. Suddenly, Miles heard a burrowing sound. "Asher, is that you?" he asked nervously.

Asher appeared on his other side. "Is what me?"

"That swishing sound," Miles replied, swapping his pickaxe for his wrench. "Sounds like a snake."

The ground shook. A snake broke through the corrupted dirt and flew out toward them. "A Devourer," Miles exclaimed, remembering what Matthew had taught him. He released his wrench, hitting the snakelike creature in the head. "Use a ranged weapon if you can." More snakes poured out and began circling.

Asher pulled out a handful of spiky balls. Miles noticed they looked exactly like the ones Isaac had thrown at the unicorns. Asher tossed them at the approaching snakes. His aim wasn't great, but every other hit destroyed a piece of an enemy. Miles repeated his wrench throws with more accuracy, but his hits were less potent. He shot the remaining snakes with the Dao of Pow, confusing them enough that he could finish them off with his yo-yo and Asher's poorly aimed explosions.

"I think we got them all," Asher said proudly. "We make a good team in a fight."

"Sure we do," Miles responded politely, though he felt he deserved more credit than his partner. "How is the underground Corruption situation?"

Asher jumped into the large pit he had dug and examined a handful of dirt. "There's one more patch of Corruption and my drill is out!" he called up. They were out of powder, too. Then he remembered the Holy Water. Isabella said it was for an emergency and this seemed like a good time to use it. He tossed the bottle down to Asher who uncorked it and purified the last bit of corrupted land. "We've done all we can for now," he called up to Miles. "Let's head back."

Miles gave him a hand getting back up and the two of them climbed to the surface. As they traveled back to the Hallow, Miles was grateful Asher wasn't in a talkative mood. Something was bothering him about Asher and he was trying to put his finger on it. He had been uncomfortable talking about his past. And he had that suspicious alien weapon from his former companion. But what was bothering Miles most was the spiky balls. The Tinkerer had always kept a stash ready to toss in a fight. Asher had disappeared right when Isaac was taken down. Could Asher have taken Isaac's weapons after he was killed, or even before? Miles didn't like being suspicious, but Asher was not making it easy to trust him.

# Chapter 12
## THE RETURN OF THE FROST LEGION

Miles and Asher made their way back to the Hallow, appreciating the changes they made in the landscape with their hard work. As Asher chatted about their daring mission and narrow escape, Miles found it harder to keep his suspicions to himself. That, combined with the fact that he had finished all the snacks he had packed for the journey, was making him very grumpy.

"I'll bet that's the last of the Corruption," Asher said confidently.

"You'd lose all your coins with a bet like that." Miles sighed. "We're going to need a lot more Purification Powder to rid this world of Corruption. And it's totally unfair that we need to use what we earned to pay for the Purification Powder to get rid of the Corruption. Everyone benefits from it but only we have to pay."

Asher nodded in agreement. "I hear you loud and clear, Miles. It's not fair that you do all the work and make all the sacrifices but everyone gains from it. That's why I got out of the game and became an adventurer. I travel alone and take care of myself," he said proudly. Miles thought it was probably the most honest thing he had ever heard Asher say.

As they approached the Hallow, a message appeared: "The Frost Legion has arrived." Miles and Asher broke into a run to warn the others. "The Frost Legion is back! Weapons ready, everyone!"

"You know how to make a grand entrance!" Sarah called out as Miles ran past her.

"Stick with me, Stylist. You'll never be bored!" Miles called back as he ran up the tree house steps to grab his Mythril Armor, Palladium Repeater, and Cobalt weapons he had crafted ages ago. He was excited to be able to finally put them to good use. Fighting these snowmen was getting a little routine with his old tools.

He threw open the storage chest, but all he found in the inventory was a pair of binoculars and a bone feather, neither of which were his.

Miles slammed his fist on the lid. "Stolen! I can't believe it!" He heard a commotion from below and looked out the window. The Frost Legion had arrived.

This was the most dangerous legion yet, and he had to get down there, even if he had lame weapons.

He arrived in the thick of the battle as his friends were already throwing wrenches, fireballs, explosives and other projectiles at the snowmen. He felt proud to be a member of this team of dedicated fighters, and even more proud to be considered its leader. He looked over and saw Asher slashing at snowmen with better aim than he had shown in the past. On closer inspection, the sword actually looked like the Beam Sword the armored skeleton had dropped when he and Sarah defeated him.

*That proves he's a thief,* Miles thought. *That sword was mine.* The thought made him angry. Angrier than he had ever been. In a rage, he brought his broadsword down, hacking at every snowman that moved. He then took out his wrench and shot it into the oncoming crowd, taking out five or six with each throw.

When the fight was over, a message appeared. "The Frost Legion has been defeated."

"It's about time those things stopped coming around," Asher said, carefully placing the sword back into his inventory. He saw Miles looking at him and recognition flashed across his face. Asher could tell Miles was angry and he didn't seem surprised. Asher dusted himself off and announced,

"Well, if that's done, I'm off to mine for some potions. Back in a bit!" Then he dashed off.

Without a word, Miles followed him.

"Hey, where ya goin'? Miles, I can give you that makeover now!"

"Maybe later, Sarah. I have some business to attend to," Miles replied as he stalked after Asher.

He didn't have to travel far before he saw Asher in a clearing. He was lying on a rock, hands behind his head and looking at the sky as if he didn't have a care in the world. He jumped up as he heard Miles come near. "Who's there?"

Miles was still so angry, he didn't trust himself to speak. He stood there and waited for Asher to notice him. Asher put his hand up to shield his eyes from the sun. "Oh, hi Miles! What's up?"

"I'd like to see your sword please," Miles demanded.

"Which one? I have a few," Asher answered.

"The Beam Sword," Miles said quietly. "The one you were fighting the Frost Legion with."

"Oh, is that what it is? It's a nifty little thing. Glows, too," Asher said, trying to sound casual as he took the sword from his inventory and handed it to Miles. "Bought it off a Goblin a while back."

Miles examined the sword. It looked exactly like the one he had gotten in the cave. He flicked the sword toward a tree and a bullet came flying out.

"I had no idea it could do that," Asher said, clearly surprised.

"You bought it and didn't even know what it could do?" Miles challenged him. "You're smarter than that, Asher. I think you're craftier than you let on."

"And you're smarter than I thought you were," Asher said. He jumped to his feet and grabbed the sword from Miles. "I'll take that back, thanks." Asher pointed the sword at Miles. "I try to stay away from danger, if you couldn't tell."

Miles cursed himself for not being ready for an attack. He drew his broadsword and clashed it against the Beam Sword Asher was holding. "You stole that from me."

"You can't prove anything. It's in my inventory and I say I got it from a Goblin. It's your word—or sword—against mine." Asher began dueling with Miles. He was more skilled at this type of combat than with ranged weapons, Miles noticed.

"Cut it out, Asher. I don't want to hurt you. I just want my weapons back and I want you to leave. I promise if you do that, I won't come after you."

"Why would I leave?" Asher asked, grinning. "I have a nice home in the Hallow, and good friends, all thanks to you. But now I don't need you anymore. If you leave, I won't have to hurt you."

Miles jumped up onto a rock and tried to win an advantage over Asher as they continued their sword fight. "You talk a big game, Asher, but you're all talk, no game."

Asher whirled to avoid Miles's blade, but he stumbled and the broadsword blade cut his shoulder. "Ouch! That hurt!" Asher exclaimed.

Miles realized he was getting the best of him. Asher was hurt and his attacks were getting slower and sloppier. Miles kept up his steady stream of hits against Asher's sword. He didn't want to hurt the guy. Miles only wanted to defend himself. Asher held up a hand. "Can we call time out for a second?" He was panting.

"Time out? Who calls time out in a battle?" Miles replied, but he held up his sword for a moment. "But if you need a time out, I'll resume beating you in a few moments."

"Thanks, pal. I'm thirsty." Asher pulled a potion bottle from his inventory and downed it, becoming instantly invisible. "Ahh," said Asher's disembodied voice. "That's much better. See ya!" Asher's voice and footsteps faded away.

Mile picked up the discarded Beam Sword and wiped it clean, placed it in his inventory. *For once, I'm not happy that I was right*, he thought as he headed off to break the bad news to his friends.

# Chapter 13
## BACK IN THE HALLOW

Miles was happy to find that everyone was together back at the Hallow. They were seated at the long dining room table he had crafted when he built the extra rooms. Sarah was the first to notice his arrival.

"You can't avoid that makeover forever, you know," Sarah joked, making room for him at the table. "I know where you live now."

Autumn looked past Miles. "Where's Asher? Didn't you leave with him?"

Miles snorted. "Yeah, more like tracked him down and exposed him."

"I know you've never trusted him, but aren't you being a little dramatic?" Isabella asked. She had such a trusting nature. Miles felt bad telling her the truth, but he had to be honest. It was the only way of protecting them all.

"He stole my sword. The one I got with Sarah in the cave," Miles explained. "I went after Asher to give him a chance to explain where he got it, but he attacked me."

"Where is he now?" John asked.

Miles shrugged and laughed. "I have no idea. He could be here in this room right now."

Everyone looked around, confused. Jack even looked under the table.

"Invisibility potion, eh?" Cedric asked. "He bought that from me before you left. Said it was his favorite escape route."

"Yeah, I was beating him in a sword fight but he called time out."

"You can't call time out in a sword fight!" Jack shouted.

"Agreed," Miles said. "When he called time out, he drank the potion, disappeared and that's literally the last I saw of the guy."

Autumn was trying not to laugh, but she couldn't help herself. "So you're a great warrior and you get taken by the oldest magic trick in the book?"

Miles laughed along with her. "I never said I was perfect. But I also told you guys I didn't get a good feeling from him. Many of you were suspicious of him, too!"

Isabella looked like she was about to cry. "Why would he turn on you like that?"

Miles shrugged again. "I don't understand what the guy is up to. Sometimes he's helpful, generous and happy to be here. But he took my sword and . . ." Miles didn't want to accuse him without evidence, but everything pointed in his direction. "He may have stolen other weapons, too."

"That's a big accusation. Do you have any proof?" John asked.

"I don't," Miles admitted. "But I can't worry about him now. I can only warn you all against Asher and caution you not to trust him. We have the Corruption to fight." He turned to Isabella. "So, Dryad, how are we doing against the Corruption?"

Isabella closed her eyes and reached out with her mind. A smile flickered across her face. "There is more good in the world than bad." She opened her eyes. "The fight is almost complete."

Miles smiled with relief. It was the first good news in a long time. "So I can take a break and hang out with my friends for a while?"

Isabella shook her head. "If you wait too long, the Corruption will return."

"I was afraid you'd say that," Miles said with a sigh. "How much Purification Powder can I get for these coins?"

"It'll cost all you have," Autumn said, looking at his inventory. "You can't spend everything you have on the powder."

"I can get more coins later," Miles said with resolve. "It's the only way we can be rid of the Corruption for good."

Isabella handed him the powder. John placed a delicious-smelling meal on the table for Miles. "You'll have to keep up your strength. Eat something before you go."

Miles mumbled his thanks and dug in, eating heartily. "This is terrific," he said through a mouth full of pumpkin pie.

"You're supposed to eat the meal before dessert," Sarah chided him.

"Pumpkin's a vegetable. I'll have the shrimp and soup for dessert," Miles smiled through a mouthful of pie.

"You can be so gross sometimes," Autumn said.

"You should see him when he takes out enemies with a severed zombie arm!" Sarah replied, laughing. "Now that's gross!"

Despite the bad news about Asher, the atmosphere at the dinner table was actually relaxed and fun. They joked, laughed, told each other stories about how they met Miles and about their first impressions of each other. Miles loved how quickly his new friends had become old friends, and he was sad that he had to leave them so soon.

He packed up the best weapons Asher hadn't stolen and took leftover food from dinner (mostly more pumpkin pie). He made sure his chests were locked, and double-checked his stock of Purification Powder. "I think I have everything," he said as he prepared to leave. One by one, his companions shook his hand or crushed him in a hug. Then, wiping a tear from his eye that he hoped no one saw, he took off to find and fight the Corruption.

Miles tramped through the desert and hit a snowy landscape next, amazed that a dry cactus could exist next to ice and cold. He looked around nervously. "Where there's snow, there must be a snowman," he said out loud to the cold evening air. His breath escaped from his mouth like fog, and he watched it puff into tiny white clouds for a few breaths before he realized it was snowing. Beautiful flakes were falling from the sky. Despite the cold, this was Miles's favorite biome so far. It was quiet and still.

Night was falling and he still had far to travel. Miles lit a torch to keep out the darkness. As he walked, he had the sense someone was following him. He looked back and saw someone bundled up in thick armor a few paces behind.

Shuffle, shuffle. Groan.

Miles assumed it was a zombie. The time of day was right and the sounds were a match. As it came closer, he realized it was actually a zombie Eskimo.

"I'm assuming all zombies are built the same way," Miles said to the rotting creature as it shuffled toward him. He pulled out his Beam Sword and tried it out on the approaching zombie. *Zap!* It glowed, lighting up the area and shooting a bullet straight at the zombie.

"Easy kill," Miles said happily, picking up the rare Eskimo armor drop and set of coins. The armor needed airing out—it reeked of decaying zombie flesh—but it would be useful if Miles planned to spend any more time in the snow.

The white snow turned purple as Miles reached the edge of the Corruption. Miles was sad to see it had darkened the beautiful snow and he vowed to see it clean again. He walked as he blew the powder across the landscape, annoyed that he had Asher to thank for this new technique. He reached the end of the biome as it turned to jungle and was amazed to see the jungle was lush and green—not an inch of Corruption anywhere, and he still had powder left.

Miles dug where the Corruption had ended and sprinkled powder on the few purple spots he had missed. He went back to the other edge where the Corruption had made its first bruise on the snow and dug there as well, carefully searching for signs of purple. Even one leftover block could spread and take over the land again.

Miles wiped his brow, surprised that he was sweating in the icy cold of the snow biome. Miles hoped he had the time and strength to get back to the Hallow. He had done his part, restoring balance. Now it was up to others to keep it away. He had earned a rest.

# Chapter 14
## YOU'RE A SLIME

As Miles neared the Hallow, he heard arguing coming from the house. He looked up and saw Sarah holding a breakable pot, ready to throw it at someone. Miles rushed to the tree house. When he got to the landing, he saw that someone was Asher!

"You have some nerve coming back here!" Miles shouted.

Isabella stood between Sarah and Asher. "I think you should listen to what Asher had to say," she said.

"Why? He stole my sword and tried to kill me!" Miles practically screamed at Isabella.

Asher held up his hands in protest. "That was a misunderstanding," he said.

Just then, they heard shouts coming from down below. "Shoo! Shoo! Get them out of here! They're ruining my potions!" Cedric yelled. They all ran down to see slimes hopping up and down, surrounding poor Cedric. "They won't leave me alone!"

"I've got this," Asher said, pulling out a familiar Cobalt Sword. He slashed at the slimes, killing off the entire invasion. All the companions could do was watch in awe. The sword was so fast, so efficient, so beautiful. And it belonged to Miles.

As Asher slew the final Slime with a satisfying splat, Miles rushed at him angrily. Asher stopped him, holding up the Cobalt weapon. "Not so fast," Asher teased. "This is one powerful blade. You don't want to have an accident with it."

"That is my sword and you know it!" Miles shouted.

Asher laughed. "Of course I know it. I took it from your chest. You know, you should keep your weapons locked up. You're far too trusting."

"So you admit it?" Sarah said, standing next to Miles in a show of support.

"Yes, I do. Now that the balance is restored and I have these awesome weapons, you're no use to me anymore."

Isabella burst into tears. "But we trusted you!" she cried. John and Cedric went to comfort her.

Jack and Autumn went to stand by Miles and Sarah. "Leave. *now*!" Jack ordered Asher.

"Not before I get my weapons back," Miles growled.

# Chapter 15
## ICE MELTS

Miles woke up in the house in the Hallow, surrounded by his friends. And Asher. "What's *he* doing here?" Miles demanded. He sounded weaker than he had hoped he would.

"It's okay," Autumn said. "He's here to apologize."

"I am," Asher said softly. "I took it too far."

"You destroyed me. With my own sword. Too far doesn't begin to cover it," Miles said, trying to sit up.

Asher sat on the side of Miles's bed. "I've been a bad friend. You don't deserve anything I did. I am sorry. This is what I've been doing for a long time, making friends with people to take advantage of them. I've never been ashamed until now."

"Why now?" Sarah demanded.

"Because you're so nice. You're not just companions; you're family. Many groups help each other for their own gain, but you care for each other." Asher bowed his head. "At first it made me angry. I tried to come up with a plan to punish you for being so good. I had to wait until you defeated the Corruption, Miles, and while I waited, I carried out my plans to make your friends like me better and then get rid of you."

"What changed your mind?" Miles asked.

"All of you. When I was invisible, I followed Miles back here and watched you at dinner, laughing and having a good time. I wanted that. At first, I thought I'd have to do away with Miles and replace him. Sorry about that, pal," Asher said as an aside to Miles. "But as soon as I beat you, I realized I had done a terrible thing. I had gotten rid of my first real friend." Asher began to sob. "I only hope you can forgive me."

"That was a nice speech," Miles said. "But you'll have to do a lot better than make a speech to gain our trust."

Asher nodded. "I understand." He took a large pouch of coins from his inventory and handed it over to Isabella.

"What's this for?" she asked.

"Purification Powder. It should be enough to stop the Corruption for good." Asher spread his hands wide. "All I have is my coins and my word, but I'll do everything I can to prove that you can trust me."

Isabella opened the pouch and poured the coins onto the bed. Her eyes opened wide in surprise. "They're all platinum. This is a fortune."

"And I'm giving it all to you so we can stop the Corruption together." Asher turned to Miles. "You spent your time and money fighting the Corruption when all you wanted was to be a great warrior. To show you how much I appreciate your sacrifice, from now on, my job is to fight the spread of the Corruption and help protect our friends. If you'll let me."

Isabella looked at Miles questioningly. "Give him the powder, I guess," Miles said. "Let's see what he does with it." Isabella doled out the powder and Asher stacked it in his inventory.

"I won't let you guys down. I promise. Miles was a great teacher. You, too, Isabella. I'm better at spreading powder and digging than I am at fighting. My griefing days are over," Asher announced.

"Speaking of digging, how *did* you get that Laser Drill?" Miles asked.

Asher smiled mischievously. "You probably don't want to know. I don't come out looking good in that story!"

Miles patted him on the back. "Perhaps when you return from spreading the powder, we can sit around a campfire and you can tell us about your adventures."

Asher smiled. "It's a plan." He headed to the door. "I'll see you soon," he said to the group. "And that's a promise, not a threat!"

"Be safe," Isabella called out.

# Chapter 16
# NEW ADVENTURES

hope we can trust him," Autumn said, watching Asher leave.

"We'll know soon enough," Miles said. "Isabella can keep an eye on the balance to track his progress."

"And you can go off to become a fearless warrior," Jack said.

"Yes," Miles agreed. "But I realize I have apologies to make, too. I behaved badly through parts of this journey. I was braggy and immature and impatient at times. I wanted to battle and get ahead, not just cure the Corruption. I was wrong."

His friends nodded quietly.

"Hey, wait a second." Miles suddenly realized something else. "The dude still has my weapons!"

Just then, Cedric walked in. "Young Miles? The adventurer asked me to show you something. Come."

"Hey, you remembered my name!" Miles said happily as he followed Cedric downstairs.

Cedric held up his hand. Miles's name was written on his palm. "The adventurer said it bothered you when I forgot your name, so he wrote it here."

"So you'll remember my name until you wash your hand?" Miles asked.

"That is most likely true!" Cedric laughed.

Cedric led Miles to a large chest at the base of a tree. "The adventurer left it for you. I can't recall his name, though. He didn't write it down."

Miles opened the chest to find all of his weapons and armor, along with a set of Adamantite Armor—some of the strongest armor in Terraria. There was also a note, which said simply: "Go get 'em, Miles. I'll be rooting for you!"

Miles put on the armor. It was light and strong and fit perfectly.

"You don't even need a makeover now," Sarah said. "You look perfectly fearless."

"Thanks, Sarah, but I could use a haircut, if you still want to give me one."

Sarah sat Miles down on a nearby tree stump and styled his hair, then took him to look at his reflection in a bucket of water. "You look sharp, if I may say so myself."

"I do look good," Miles said, admiring his reflection. "Thanks." He handed her a coin but she pushed it back toward him.

"We're friends," she said. "Besides, you're much easier to look at now that you're not all scruffy." She laughed. Miles laughed along with her.

Miles found John looking through the weapons chest. "These are sweet weapons, Miles. What do you plan on doing with them?" he asked.

Miles didn't hesitate. "There's one foe I've heard of—the Destroyer. He looks like the Eater of Worlds but he's made of metal, won't break apart, and shoots lasers." Jack whistled with appreciation. "Now that I have this armor and my weapons, I think I can take him on. At least, I'd like to try."

Jack searched Miles's inventory. "Let's see. Your Dao of Pow will be useful, along with this Repeater. This Cobalt Shield will pair nicely with a Star Cloak—you'll have to seek out a Mimic if you don't have one already."

"My Meteor Staff will be a huge help," Miles, turned to Jack. "What else do you think I will need?"

"Well, you'll need some healing potions or a nurse on staff during the fight," Jack replied. "Some fireworks would kill it with practically no combat, and it would look spectacular . . ."

"I don't think I'll use explosives or fireworks. I want a fair fight, me against the Destroyer. It's the best way to become a true warrior," Miles explained.

"Although I love a good explosion, I respect your approach," Jack said.

John walked over, looking businesslike. "I hear you may need some healing potion."

Miles nodded. "I'm off to face my next foe, and I hear he's a tough one."

"It's the Destroyer, right?" John held out a stack of healing potion. "Take this. My gift to you."

Miles was surprised by his offer. "But you're a merchant. You don't usually give things away for free."

John hugged him. "You have given us so much. There is no way any of us could repay you. Please take the potion." John continued, "I have a lot to gain if you come back a rich man because you defeated one of the hardest mobs in all of Terraria!"

Miles smiled. "Well in that case, I'll take it. But be prepared with a good stock of merchandise for when I come back. I'm going to need lots of new supplies!"

Miles walked over to where Isabella was searching the map. "How is the Corruption holding off?"

Isabella studied the map for longer than usual. Miles was beginning to worry when a big smile spread across her face. "Our world is almost completely pure. You have done well!"

"And Asher?" Miles asked nervously.

"He has been spreading the powder and digging trenches, just as you directed. And he has even filled in trenches where the Corruption is no longer a threat."

"Then I'm safe to go off on my next journey?" Miles asked.

"Yes, Miles. Go and live your dream." The dryad kissed him on the cheek.

Miles gathered his supplies and readied himself. They all gathered at the edge of the Hallow to say goodbye.

"Good-bye, everyone! And thank you for everything!" Miles said.

"Good-bye, Miles!" they all replied.

"Be safe. Terraria needs you!" Isabella called to him.

With a wave and a smile, Miles set off on his next adventure, hoping to return a warrior.

"You'll have to fight me for them," Asher replied, holding up the Cobalt Sword. "You're no match for me."

Miles pulled out his trusty broadsword and clashed weapons with Asher. Their skills were evenly matched, but Asher's sword had more power and speed.

"I hope this teaches you a lesson," Asher said as he swung at Miles, grazing his leg. Miles thrust his sword at Asher. Asher ducked away and countered with a blow to Miles's head. Miles reeled back in pain and white spots danced in front of his eyes. As he lay on the ground, he looked up to see Asher standing above him.

"Guess that means I win," Asher said, grinning. Miles tried to reply, but everything went dark. He had been defeated with his own sword.